The Book of
Thanksgiving

The Book of
Thanksgiving

Paul Dickson

A Perigee Book

A Perigee Book
Published by The Berkley Publishing Group
200 Madison Avenue
New York, NY 10016

Book design by Joseph F. Perez
Cover design by James R. Harris
Cover illustration by Betsy Franco Feeney

First edition: November 1995

Published simultaneously in Canada.

Library of Congress Cataloging-in-Publication Data

Dickson, Paul.
    The book of Thanksgiving / Paul Dickson. — 1st ed.
        p.   cm.
    "A Perigee book."
    ISBN 0-399-52163-1 (pbk.)
    1. Thanksgiving Day.   2. Thanksgiving cookery.   I. Title.
GT4975.D53   1995   95-7694
394.2'649—dc20   CIP

Printed in the United States of America.

10 9 8 7 6 5 4 3 2 1

This book is printed on acid-free paper.

CONTENTS

ACKNOWLEDGMENTS

THE FIRST DRAFT of this book was finished on Thanksgiving eve, 1993, which was an appropriate moment to thank those who made it possible:

James Baker, Paula Fisher, and Carolyn Travers of Plimoth Plantation; Connie Garcia of Ocean Spray Cranberries Inc.; Deidre Goguen of Old Sturbridge Village; Bill Hickman, Bobbi Kadesh, and Jeffrey LaFleur of the Cranberry Institute: Cape Cod Cranberry Growers Association; Elizabeth L. Newhouse, Maxine Rapoport, Doris and Mike Feinsilber, and Bob Skole.

"Thanksgiving! What a world of pleasant memories the word recalls. Memories obscured and softened not by the mists of time, but by the fragrant steam rising slowly from innumerable savory dishes! Oh the Thanksgiving dinners we have eaten! The Thanksgiving cheer of which we have partaken."

—John Tremain, Victorian writer

INTRODUCTION

"Thanksgiving . . . is the one day that is purely American."

—O. Henry

 IF YOU LOVE Thanksgiving, this is the book for you. If I may mix my holiday metaphors, this book is a Valentine to Thanksgiving.

If, however, you are at the extremity of political correctness and think that Thanksgiving should be frowned upon, that Thanksgiving pageants should be banned from the public schools, that the day be declared a day of mourning for the turkey, that Squanto and Priscilla Mullin have been shamelessly exploited by history, you have come to the wrong place.

In 1993 a *Washington Post* Thanksgiving editorial noted forces trying to dim the occasion—"from those who annually condemn the day's carnivorous fare to critics who view American history as a tale of unrelieved rapine and plunder followed by overeating and football"—and essentially told such naysayers to get with the program, to whine about something else.

Criticism of Thanksgiving is nothing new. For all of his other virtues, Thomas Jefferson somehow got it in his head that Thanksgiving was a "monarchical practice" and refused to observe it.

In the late 1950s Dr. Francis Mason, professor of English at Gettysburg College, made newspaper headlines by calling the wire services and demanding a new kind of Thanksgiving free of "false practices and all their sentimental symbols."

His rallying cry was, "Let's have no more Pilgrim fathers lugging fat turkeys out of the forest primeval, their muskets cocked for hungry Indians, under the benediction of the harvest moon." Mason called for a number of reforms including: "No more confusing the gentle glow of honest fellowship with the animal heat of a full stomach. . . . No more provincial pride masquerading as Christian righteousness . . . No more Governors' proclamations or other civic substitutes for prayer . . . No more annual orgies of commercialism and self-indulgence . . ." After this came the windup as the Day was labeled "a farce in the name of national worship," and Mason ended with this ill-tempered and genuinely nasty conclusion: "To find untroubled satisfaction in the enjoyment of good things which are denied to our neighbors is a perversion of Christian logic and a mockery of Christian love."

It gets worse. In the late 1960s our shoot-from-the-hip pop psychologists began to fill newspaper columns on the stress and strain of the day. Dr. Joyce Brothers told us all on Thanksgiving Eve 1968 that "the dream of family unity and relaxed feasting has a way of disintegrating into bickering and disgruntled feelings, as the family accord is too much of a strain."

Nice! This is akin to bringing up the divorce rate on one's wedding night.

By 1991 there was so much static in the air that a writer could start an op-ed piece in the *New York Times* entitled "Multicultural Fowl" with the line: "Thanksgiving is under attack again." Trends noted here included the assertion that "Apostles of political correctness grimly insist that Thanksgiving be declared a Day of National Mourning for the Native Americans."

On the other hand, if you think the words "I'll be home for Thanksgiving" are among the finest words that can be heard (or uttered), that Norman Rockwell's depictions of the holiday are right on target, that it is a time of great merriment, that the turkey baster and carcass lifter are instruments of joy, then you will enjoy the pages which follow.

This book has one simple purpose: to help celebrate our most uncomplicated and most enjoyable day—the only holiday where we are *expected* to overeat and to doze on the couch—so this book has been organized in such a manner as to encourage dipping and browsing and moving between areas. Only the most compulsive will choose to read it straight through.

On to the issues at hand!

When—and what—was the first Thanksgiving? Was it a feast of venison and wild turkey, shared by Indians and Pilgrims in gratitude for a bountiful harvest? And if so, why was it delayed until the fourth Thursday in November? And what about all the claims from places such as Texas and Virginia?

We will answer such questions and dote and dwell on such things as the crusading suffragette editor who fought for a good part of her life to give us the modern holiday, the best toasts and graces, essential Thanksgiving definitions, words from the past, a few recipes—in short, total holiday fare.

The Pilgrims and Plymouth

"The rock [Plymouth Rock] underlies all America: it only
crops out here."

—Wendell Phillips, speech at Plymouth, Mass.,
December 21, 1855

ALTHOUGH COUNTLESS ASSUMPTIONS have been made
over the years, very little is actually known about the
1621 event in Plymouth that is the model for our
Thanksgiving. The only surviving references to the
event are quoted here.

I. The background for the first Thanksgiving is found
in Gov. William Bradford's history of Plymouth in
which he talked about the fall of 1621.

"They began now to gather in the small harvest they had, and to fit
up their house and dwelling against winter, being all well recovered
in health and strength and had all things in good plenty. For as some
were thus employed in affairs abroad, others were exercised in fishing, about cod and bass and other fish, of which they took good

store, of which every family had their portion. All the summer there was no want; and now began to come in store of fowl, as winter approached, of which this place did abound when they came first (but afterward decreased by degrees). And besides waterfowl there was great store of wild turkeys, of which they took many, besides venison, etc. Besides, they had about a peck a meal a week to a person, or now since harvest, Indian corn to that proportion. Which made many afterwards write so largely of their plenty here to their friends in England, which were not feigned but true reports."

—William Bradford, *Of Plimoth Plantation*;
S.E. Morison, ed., Knopf, N.Y., 1952, p. 90

II. The original and only account of the first Thanksgiving is contained in a letter dated December 21, 1621, from Edward Winslow in Plymouth to George Morton in England. It appeared in print in *Mourt's Relation*, published in London in 1662.

"Our harvest being gotten in, our governor sent four men on fowling, that so we might after a special manner rejoice together after we had gathered the fruit of our labors. They four in one day killed as much fowl as, with a little help beside, served the company almost a week. At which time, amongst other recreations, we exercised our arms, many of the Indians coming amongst us, and among the rest their greatest king Massasoit, with some ninety men, whom for three days we entertained and feasted, and they went out and killed five deer, which they brought to the plantation and bestowed on our governor, and upon the captain and others. And although it be not always so plentiful as it was at this time with us, yet by the goodness of God, we are so far from want that we often wish you partakers of our plenty."

—Edward Winslow, *Mourt's Relation*, D.B. Heath, ed.,
Corinth Books, N.Y., 1963, p. 82

To gather information on the first Thanksgiving the best place to go is Plimoth Plantation (as Governor Bradford spelled it) in Plymouth, Massachusetts. Today, Plimoth Plantation is the outdoor living-history museum of 17th-century Plymouth. The main exhibits are *Mayflower II*, a 1627 Pilgrim village, and a Wampanoag Indian summer campsite. Plimoth Plantation is near the town of Plymouth, just off Massachusetts Route 3, about 40 minutes south of Boston.

The late Henry Hornblower II of Boston was instrumental in getting the Plimoth reconstruction under way. In 1949, the first house went up along the waterfront with the rest of the reconstruction taking place in the 1950s. The reconstruction date of 1627 was not arbitrarily chosen. During that year Isaac de Rasieres traveled from New Amsterdam (now New York City) to visit the village and wrote a lengthy letter in Dutch describing the settlement. The reconstruction was patterned after this letter. A settlement census dated 1627 also exists, enabling reconstruction personnel to know the names and family units of that time.

The expert authority on all of this is Plimoth Plantation historian James Baker, who begins by saying that there is no specific date for the three-day celebration, but it was between September 21 and November 9.

Baker says that from the two surviving descriptions, we learn that the feast included codfish, sea bass, wild fowl (such as ducks, geese, and swans), turkeys, corn (and probably wheat) meal, and the five deer brought by Indians.

"Beyond those foods noted," says Baker, "they had a number of native and English fruits and herbs." The former were both wild and cultivated, the latter planted in the cottage gardens from English seeds. Following are the lists that the Plantation has prepared.

Native Plants

Walnuts
Chestnuts
Grapes
American and Beach Plums
Smooth and Round-leaved Gooseberries
Raspberries
Wild Cherries
Ground Nuts (*Apios Tuberosa*)
Wild Strawberries
Watercress

Beans
Pumpkins
Squash
American Crab Apples
Hickory Nuts
Currants
Blueberries
Jerusalem Artichokes
Wild Onions
Purslane

Baker notes that many of the fruits were no longer in season by harvest time but may have been served in their dried form. The English fields and gardens may not have produced abundantly, but some familiar foods would have been available. The field pea crop failed, but the barley survived and provided the colonists with malt for beer. Baker says that nobody knows for sure which English plants were set in the gardens in 1621, but we may assume that the following popular plants were being cultivated:

English Plants

Parsnips	Melons
Carrots	Radishes
Turnips	Skirrets
Onions	Beets
Cabbages	Lettuce

Beverages available to the Pilgrims included both beer and a strong brandylike liquid known as aqua vitae, literally "water of life." Milk was not consumed. Children drank beer along with their elders.

Generally speaking, meat, fish, and bread were the most important elements of the diet at this time, although fruits and "herbs" were sometimes eaten. The term "vegetables," Baker points out, was not in use at this time; edible plants were known as sallet (salad) herbs, potherbs, or roots. The popularity of salads and vegetable dishes was not great at this time.

Almost as interesting as what was served, is the list of those foods that were not.

—No apples, pears, or other fruits not native to New England (they would take years to bear after planting).

—Hence, no cider.

—No potatoes which were known to botanists. The sweet potato enjoyed a mild popularity in England among the well-to-do (it had supposed aphrodisiacal powers), but it was not available in early New England.

—No sweet corn. The corn grown by the Pilgrims and local Indians was a flint variety.

—No "Indian pudding" in its later form, as there was no molasses.

—Few if any naturally bitter-tasting cranberries might have been used in "puddings in the belly," which we know as stuffings, but not in their familiar jelly or preserves, because of the scarcity of sugar.

—No celery, which was unknown.

—Almost certainly no olives. They were imported in England, but it is quite unlikely that they came to Plymouth in 1620.

—No tea or coffee.

—Probably no shellfish because, as Baker notes, although they were plentiful and formed a large part of the Pilgrims' diet in the early years, they were looked on as poverty fare and hence not appropriate at a feast.

As for the feast itself, there were some differences in the presentation of food from what we might imagine. A dish was not prepared with the intent of allowing each person to take a portion. As at a modern potluck, each dish provided only a limited amount of food. Courses didn't proceed from soup to sweets, but tended to contain all sorts of dishes at the same time.

Folks sat at cloth-covered tables on benches and forms, with a few chairs for the more important men. They ate with knives, a few spoons, but no forks. Large linen napkins, about three feet square, were important since hands were used both to serve and to eat with. Instead of dishes, trenchers or small wooden plates were used. Baker says that the "reach and eat" style still used in the Near East is the best analogy to the eating style of the time.

Who were these people at that first feast? The people we call the Pilgrims today were English people who came to America to get away from the religious and economic problems of their time. Many were members of a Puritan sect known as the Separatists who had broken from the Church of England. They left England in 1620 and only about half of them survived the first winter.

There were about 140 people at the three-day harvest celebration, 90 Indian men and the Pilgrims. Only four adult housewives survived that first winter, and it is possible that they oversaw the cooking and preparation, with the help of the children and servants. They were Elizabeth Hopkins, Elinor Billington, Mary Brewster, and Susanna (White) Winslow.

A BAKER'S DOZEN MAJOR MYTHS OF THE FIRST THANKSGIVING

"Dr. [Samuel Eliot] Morison is presently revising the [Signification of the Pilgrims] pamphlet; and, while I would expect him to stick to historical truth, it is my hope and expectation that he will indulge in some 'flag-waving.' The difficulty of the Pilgrim Story is that there are really two stories—a true historical one and a romantic one. It is my sincere hope that Dr. Morison can write this story in such a way that it will be acceptable to both schools of thought."

—Harry Hornblower, Dec. 5, 1952

"More bunk has been written about the Pilgrims than any other subject except Columbus and John Paul Jones, not even excepting the Civil War."

—Samuel Eliot Morison

 AT OLD P.S. 27 in Yonkers, N.Y., the student body had been given the assignment of staging an old-fashioned Thanksgiving pageant replete with preadolescent Pilgrims, Indians, and younger kids in singing, but non-speaking roles as pumpkins and cranberries. We were expected to create costumes for the gala theatrical event. My grandmother was a master seamstress, and she volunteered to make all the male Pilgrim costumes, including those for my brother Peter and myself.

She got some pictures of Pilgrims out of magazines and constructed great tall hats with enormous rectangular buckles, buckled shoes and giant belts with giant buckles. The costumes were black muslin and set off with Puritan white stockings and oversized, detachable white cuffs and collars.

The Indians wore fine feather headdresses and slung blankets over their shoulders and made friendly grunting sounds, and we Pilgrims uttered dozens of thee's, thou's, and ye's and did a heck of a lot of proclaiming.

Great stuff!

All wrong!

With the help of James Baker of Plimoth Plantation, this is the time to set the record straight and debunk the thirteen major myths of Thanksgiving, as follows:

1. *That the occasion we know as the first Thanksgiving was indeed proclaimed as a solemn day of thanks.*

Reality. History does not record the reason for the decision—if in fact it was a decision rather than merely spontaneous reaction to circumstances—to hold a harvest festival rather than to proclaim a day of thanksgiving.

As for its being solemn, there is nothing to support this. One student of the holiday, Dr. George Pickering of the University of Detroit, was once asked by a reporter if the first Thanksgiving was a solemn event. "Solemn!" he retorted. "That first Thanksgiving was no solemn religious observance—it was a party, and a three-day party at that."

The solemnness would have been in 1623, when the people of Plymouth celebrated what they would have regarded as their first day of thanksgiving. To these people, a day of thanksgiving was a highly religious day, marked by attendance at church, prayers, and probably fasting. In contrast, they considered a harvest festival to be a leisurely and irregularly called event allowing for as much as three days devoted to feasting and games.

2. *That the people who celebrated that first Thanksgiving were known—then as now—as the Pilgrims.*

    Reality. "The people we know as the Pilgrims referred to themselves as the 'Old Comers' or 'First Comers,'" writes James Baker in his essay "The Origin of the Pilgrims," adding, "To their descendants and to succeeding generations in southeastern Massachusetts, they were known as the 'Forefathers' until the late 18th century. Most New Englanders saw the Plymouth colonists simply as their predecessors, men and women who had initiated the colonial adventure in the region. Beyond this, very little notice of the Plymouth forefathers was taken."

    The term "Pilgrim" did not first come into play as an alternative to "Forefather" until about the time of the American Revolution.

3. *That there was an important Proclamation to "ye" Pilgrims issued in 1623 establishing a day of Thanksgiving.*

Speaking of Pilgrims, there is this matter of the bogus "Pilgrim" proclamation which shows up all over the place—appearing, among other places, in a major book on holidays very much in print, on postcards and reproduction proclamations printed on parchment. Here is how it is presented in a recent and widely available reference book on American Holidays:

To show their gratitude to God, the Pilgrims set a day of Thanksgiving on November 29, 1623. Some authorities say that this second observance, rather than the one in 1621, was the real start of our present holiday, for it was religious as well as social. Here is the proclamation issued on that occasion:

TO ALL YE PILGRIMS

Inasmuch as the great Father has given us this year an abundant harvest of Indian corn, wheat, beans, squashes, and garden vegetables, and has made the forests to abound with game and the sea with fish and clams, and inasmuch as He has protected us from the ravages of the savages, has spared us from pestilence and disease, has granted us freedom to worship God according to the dictates of our own conscience; now, I, your magistrate, do proclaim that all ye Pilgrims, with your wives and little ones, do gather at ye meeting house, on ye hill, between the hours of 9 and 12 in the day time, on Thursday, November ye 29th of the year of our Lord one thousand six hundred and twenty-three, and the third year since ye Pilgrims landed on ye Pilgrim Rock, there to listen to ye pastor, and render thanksgiving to ye Almighty God for all His blessings.

—William Bradford
Ye Governor of ye colony

The proclamation is totally fraudulent and the experts at Plimoth Plantation have no idea where it came from, although Carolyn Travers of the research department guesses that it may be from a novel. If it is, the novelist's language left much to be desired in terms of authenticity: "the ravages of the savages," "garden vegetables," and so forth. Then there are the references to the Pilgrims, as in "ye Pilgrims landed on ye Pilgrim Rock." Then there is the Rock—pardon, "ye Rock"—which we shall get to shortly.

4. *That the Indians were invited to help give thanks.*
Reality. About 90 Indians were at the three-day feast staged by the Plymouth settlers, but nobody knows whether or not they were actually invited or just showed up—perhaps, summoned by the smell of the food. In any event, they were sent out to kill five deer which were added to the feast.

5. *That the Indians wore full feather headdresses.*
Reality. Artists and cartoonists have for reasons unclear chosen to depict

the Indians at Plymouth, the Wampanoag, as Plains Indians whose dress was much more elaborate.

6. *That the Pilgrims lived in log cabins.*

Reality. Despite many hundreds of illustrations to the contrary, the fact remains that this method of construction was not brought to America until 1638 by Swedish colonists in Delaware. The colonists in Plymouth lived in English frame houses built with squared and sawed timbers with wooden chimneys daubed with clay.

7. *That the original feast took place in November, as it does today, and that it was set as an annual harvest event.*

Reality. It was in September, early October at the latest. The present date, the fourth Thursday in November, was set by Lincoln, modified for a few years by Franklin D. Roosevelt and decreed by Congress in 1941.

A day of thanksgiving was not and would not have been set by rote custom because a successful harvest would not have been assumed in those perilous times when a bad harvest or famine would have made a mockery out of such a celebration.

8. *That these were Puritan celebrants who shied away from strong drink.*

Reality. The Plymouth settlers drank spirits in America as they had in England and Holland. There was no prohibition against the enjoyment of "strong waters" or beer, but drunkenness was not tolerated. The liquor they drank resembled modern brandy.

9. *That, as we have seen in many illustrations, a handful of Indians were seated around the first Thanksgiving tables.*
   Reality. The Indians outnumbered the Pilgrims 2:1.

10. *That the Pilgrims were armed with sturdy blunderbusses that they used to hunt.*
   Reality. They would have been totally inappropriate. According to the experts at Plimoth Plantation in their *Primer* on Thanksgiving, "Blunderbusses, originally donderbusses (thunder guns), were short-barreled, bell-mouthed riot guns used for dispelling crowds, not hunting."

11. *That Plymouth Rock is important to all of this.*
   Reality. James Baker has written on this subject in a paper entitled "The Origin of the Pilgrims": "The first and most important symbol in local lore associated with the Pilgrim Story is Plymouth Rock. The use of this famous rock, first identified as the landing place of the forefathers by Elder Thomas Faunce in 1741, lacks any confirming contemporary evidence." Although historians raised many questions concerning the location and placement of the Rock, Faunce's identification struck a responsive chord among ordinary folk. It quickly assumed considerable importance as a tangible symbol of the Pilgrims.

12. *That the Pilgrim men wore tall, wide-brimmed hats ornamented with large buckles, and long black coats. Men and women wore buckles on their shoes and hats. Women also wore black.*

Reality. According to James Baker, these were impositions of the Victorian Era. Though reverent before God, the Pilgrims did not drape themselves in black. There was a range of color among the inhabitants of Plymouth.

Decorative buckles are far-fetched and lack any basis in reality. They began showing up in paintings of Thanksgiving rendered in the late 19th century. The buckles fascinate Baker, who has a theory that when you want to create a mythological figure, you give that figure large buckles. "Who has big buckles?" he asks, answering, "Witches, leprechauns, Santa Claus and Pilgrims."

Our images of Pilgrims come in large measure from paintings such as the classic and drab painting *Pilgrims Going to Church* by George H. Boughton, which depicts a dozen somberly clad men, women, and children trudging through the snow shouldering muskets against possible Indian attack.

13. *That popcorn was on the table at the original celebration, having been brought there by* Quadequina, *brother of King Massasoit's brother.*

Reality. Popcorn as we know it was not available in 1621. What was available and what the pilgrims ate was *parched* corn, a flinty kernel which when heated to the point of bursting resembles a tough, half-popped corn and bears no resemblance to the large, fluffy kernels we associate with true popcorn.

James Baker addresses the issue of how this story gained a foothold: "Nineteenth-century writers, familiar with both parched corn and true popcorn, chose to use the term popcorn loosely and create a dramatic, if fictional, effect by stating that popcorn was eaten at the famous festival. The result is that modern readers who are not familiar with old parched corn are now misled into thinking our familiar movie theater treat put in its first appearance with the Pilgrims in 1621."

The line that may have started it all comes from a novel. *Standish of Standish* by Jane G. Austen, published in Boston in 1889, contained this line: "Quadequina with an amiable smile nodded to one of his attendants, who produced and poured upon the table something like a bushel of popped corn—a dainty thereto unseen and unknown by most of the Pilgrims."

The popcorn story has exploded and become fluffier over time. In 1980, the *Washington Star* gave this account: "Indians who often brought deerskin bags of popped corn to peace negotiations with English colonists, offered popcorn to the Pilgrims at their first Thanksgiving dinner, and apparently it was a big hit. Colonial settlers often ate it for breakfast with cream and sugar."

As if this wasn't enough, lines like this from a major newspaper are now beginning to show up in articles about popcorn: "Columbus found the Indians wearing popcorn decorations."

> "Blest be those feasts, with simple plenty crowned.
>   Where all the ruddy family around
>   Laugh at the jests and pranks that never fail
>   Or sigh with pity at some mournful tale."

—Oliver Goldsmith, *The Traveller*

THE ROOTS OF THANKSGIVING

"Come ye thankful people, come.
Raise the song of Harvest Home:
All is safely gathered in,
Ere the winter storms begin:

"God our maker doth provide,
For our wants to be supplied;
Come to God's own temple come
Raise the song of Harvest Home."

—Song of Harvest

THANKSGIVING, PROBABLY OUR most beloved holiday, is also the most misunderstood. The day we love to observe—with turkey with all the trimmings, family reunions and extraordinary feats of travel derring-do—originated more with one Victorian editor than Pilgrim fathers.

In fact, there is not one scintilla of evidence to suggest that Gov. William Bradford ever planned or intended for the original three-day harvest festival held in 1621 to be repeated.

Our Thanksgiving Day is the blend of three earlier traditions. The first is the New England custom of rejoicing after a successful harvest, based on earlier English harvest festivals. Following a traditional autumn feast of the Druids, the Anglo-Saxons held their "harvest home" celebration, the high point of the successful agricultural year in rural districts. As the last cartload of grain was being brought in from the fields, reapers and other workers followed the wagon, singing:

> "Harvest home, harvest home,
>   We have plowed and we have sowed,
>   We have reaped, we have mowed,
>   We have brought home every load,
>   Hip, hip, hip, harvest home!"

After the storing of grain there was a hearty supper—sometimes served in the barn—for all the farm workers. There were "substantial viands" and a superabundance of ale, with the master and mistress presiding over the festivities while receiving numerous toasts from their subjects.

This was one of the traditions brought to America, and it typified the first Thanksgiving, which was a harvest feast rather than a religious day. "The first Thanksgiving, held in Plymouth in 1621, has become enshrined in an American institution. In the seventeenth century, New England observed many days of rejoicing, but not in imitation of this original; all were ordered 'pro temporibus et causis,' according to the manner in which providence was dealing with the land," wrote noted historian Perry Miller in *The New England Mind*.

This was a harvest festival akin to the old harvest home festivals set only when there was something to celebrate. Miller points out that not only was this Thanksgiving not set as an annual event but that it would have made no sense: "For the Puritan mind, to fix thanksgiving to a mechanical revolution of the calendar would be folly; who can say that in November there will be that for which thanks should be uttered rather than lamentation?"

The second tradition comes from religious observations combining prayer and fasting, which could be proclaimed at any time of the year for special acts of divine favor or deliverance. In 1665 Connecticut through the Court of Public Records appointed a solemn day of Thanksgiving to be kept throughout the colony on the last Wednesday of October "for the blessing of the fruits of the earth and the general health of the plantations."

These were serious affairs marked by fasting, not feasting, and they were common among the early settlers, including the people we call the Pilgrims today.

Finally, the third influence was the commemoration of the landing of the Pilgrims, known in Massachusetts as Forefathers' Day. It was about this same time, in the late 18th century, that the commemoration of the Pilgrims came into play as part of Thanksgiving. Fascination and interest in the Pilgrims as historic figures began shortly before the American Revolution. They were seen as the embodiment of the national spirit and served the needs of an emerging nation that needed heroes.

The Old Colony Club was founded in Plymouth in January 1769 and had instituted an annual speech and dinner in December to honor the original settlers and their deeds. Forefathers' Day was celebrated regularly not only in Plymouth, but also in Boston and New York.

About the middle of the century, the popularity of Forefathers' Day began to decline, as the importance of Thanksgiving grew. Music, literature, and popular art of the 19th century had concentrated on the Pilgrims' landing and their first encounters with the Indians. In the late 19th century, representations of the Pilgrims began to reflect a shift of interest to the 1621 harvest celebration. That event which we now call the "First Thanksgiving" came to symbolize the union of prosperity and brotherhood.

Thus, Thanksgiving and the Pilgrims have become synonymous. As for that original Thanksgiving, listen to Dr. Kendra Stearns O'Donnell's remarks from a lecture on the real story of Thanksgiving: "The thanks given at the first Thanksgiving were, above all, for mere survival . . . Disease, starvation, accidents and perhaps even suicide marked the terrible times that gave birth to the first Thanksgiving. Governor Bradford's own wife drowned, falling overboard from the ship anchored for weeks off the bleak New England coast. It is easy to speculate, as some have, that she could not face the life that awaited her. The Indians of the area had been decimated by a great pestilence three years before the Pilgrims arrived, with terrible consequences politically, socially, economically. In one place the settlers found the ground littered with the skulls and bones of Indians: no one in that village had been left alive to bury the dead."

The first recorded formal Thanksgiving proclamation was that of Charlestown, Mass., in 1676. From 1777 to 1783 the Continental Congress and its successor, the United States Congress, issued seven proclamations. They were marked by religious fervor. References to the Revolutionary War predominated—such as the gratitude of 1780 to "His watchful providence in rescuing the person of our Commander in Chief and the Army from imminent dangers, at a moment when treason was ripened for execution."

The first national day of Thanksgiving was declared by the Continental Congress to be observed on December 18, 1777, in the hope that states would refrain from declaring their own, regional thanksgiving celebrations on different days. It was, however, a singular Thanksgiving staged to celebrate the stunning victory over the British at Saratoga. In the Continental Congress, Samuel Adams arose to declare that this electrifying victory called for a national day of Thanksgiving.

Sam Adams himself wrote the proclamation setting Thursday, December 18, as a day of "Thanksgiving and praise." The Continental Congress passed it on November 1, and the President of Congress signed it on November 7. For the first time the entire 13 colonies joined in a national day of prayer and feasting. Only one group did not participate wholeheartedly in the celebration: the soldiers of George Washington's Continental Army. They had already bivouacked just outside Philadelphia, in a place called Valley Forge.

"This is Thanksgiving Day," Lt. Col. Henry Dearborn of New Hampshire wrote in his diary on December 18. "But God knows we have very little to keep it with, this being the third day we have been without flour or bread and are living on a high uncultivated hill, in huts and tents, lying on the cold ground. Upon the whole I think all we have to be Thankful for is that we are alive and not in the grave with many of our friends." At one point in January, almost every third man was a hospital case. For one entire week, there was literally nothing in the commissary. It was only the common soldier's faith in Washington that prevented the army's complete disintegration.

On September 25, 1789, Elias Boudinot, member from New Jersey, rose up in the newly formed National Congress and presented a resolution reading: "That a joint committee of both Houses be directed to wait upon the President of the United States, to request that he would recommend to the people of the United States, a day of public Thanksgiving and prayer, to be observed by acknowledging with grateful hearts the many signal favors of Almighty God, especially by affording them an opportunity peaceably to establish a Constitution of government for their safety and happiness."

One would hardly expect such a resolution to meet with opposition, but there was vigorous debate on the subject. Edanus Burke of South Carolina was one who objected. He claimed that this was a mimicking of European customs. Thomas Tucker, also from South Carolina, protested as well, saying that the President had no right to demand that the nation offer thanks for a constitution that hadn't been tested yet and might not be satisfactory. Another felt that Thanksgiving was the business of the states and that the all-powerful Federal government should not meddle (a sentiment that has recurred in Congressional argument from that day to the present). However, the resolution was finally adopted by both houses, and President Washington issued the First National Thanksgiving Proclamation setting Thursday, November 26th, 1789, as the day. The Proclamation began as follows:

"Whereas it is the duty of all nations to acknowledge the providence of Almighty God, to obey his will, to be grateful for his benefits, and humbly to implore his protection and favor; and whereas both Houses of Congress have, by their joint Committee, requested me to recommend to the people of the United States a day of Public Thanksgiving and Prayer, to be observed by acknowledging with grateful hearts the many and signal favors of Almighty God, especially by affording them an opportunity peaceably to establish a form of government for their safety and happiness."

But Thanksgiving did not prove immediately popular outside of New England. John Jay, governor of New York, attempted to set a statewide day of Thanksgiving in 1785, but met with little success. The custom was allowed to lapse during the administration of Thomas Jefferson, who saw proclamations of thanksgiving as "monarchical practice." But on April 13, 1815, President James Madison called for a day of thanksgiving to celebrate the end of the War of 1812.

Meanwhile in New England, Thanksgiving was becoming a popular time for weddings. Research conducted by historians at Old Sturbridge Village points out that by the 1830s, rural marriages still followed seasonable rhythms, with couples taking vows in either the early spring or after the harvest in November or December. With families gathered together, Thanksgiving was a favorite time chosen by brides, who were traditionally married at home. Wedding anniversaries were also counted among the day's blessings.

Thanksgiving also meant back to school for 1830s children. With the harvest complete, students would attend the district school throughout the winter, from about December through March. The holiday marked the boundary between the seasons of hard work, which left little time for large social gatherings, and winter. As the temperatures fell, many routine farming chores would be dropped, leaving more time for leisure. Thus the day of annual Thanksgiving became well established in much of New England.

Then Thanksgiving began moving west. In 1844 the territory of Iowa, for instance, found enough to be thankful for that its first official Thanksgiving holiday was proclaimed on October 12 by Governor John Chambers, to be observed on December 12. The *Davenport Gazette* of November 21, 1844, was of the opinion that "former residents of New England" would rejoice in learning that the Governor had introduced the "time-honored custom" west of the Mississippi. "May it long prevail with due observance," the *Gazette* concluded. The *Iowa City Standard* was glad to welcome "the good old Pilgrim custom to our midst." In 1846 it was moved to the last Thursday in November.

An event that occurred in 1859 suggests a less than universal love of the idea of Thanksgiving and, in fact, some fear of it. The city of Washington, D.C. had a slate of aldermen who voted 7–5 to ban Thanksgiving on the basis that it promoted "drunkenness and disorder," and, to make matters worse, it was cited as "a creation of New England people." These were tense days. John Brown was in jail awaiting execution for his raid on the Federal armory at Harper's Ferry. Brown had staged his daring raid to get arms for his war on slavery. Some in Washington felt that the New Englanders would use the day to make "incendiary harangues." The mayor of the District of Columbia, however, overruled the ban by the "gloomy aldermen," and on the day after Thanksgiving, November 25, the editor of the *Washington Star* was able to report, "The weather yesterday was truly delicious. . . . We saw no one, young or old, positively intoxicated."

All of this is fine, but does not address the question of why Thanksgiving lands on Thursday. James Baker says that it had to fall on a weekday because it could not conflict with the Sabbath. Thanksgiving usually fell on the weekday set aside as "Lecture Day," which was a combination of a midweek church meeting and market day. This fell on Wednesday in Connecticut but on Thursday in Massachusetts.

There was also the matter of "fish days" in early America. A fish day was one when you couldn't eat meat. Elizabeth I of England wanted to boost the fishing business in her country and so decreed that people couldn't eat meat on Wednesdays, Fridays and Saturdays. Settlers in Plymouth and Boston, though not bound by that old rule, nonetheless were influenced by it. They tended to fast often, particularly on Wednesdays, Fridays and Saturdays. But they decided to make Thursday their market day, when they'd trade their goods in town and stock up.

Thursday became the big meat, feast market and meeting day, so when the civic authorities declared a day of thanksgiving, it was on Thursday. The exception was in colonial Connecticut, where Thanksgiving was on Wednesday. The Massachusetts way of doing things won out when Thanksgiving went from being a regional holiday to a national holiday.

THE WOMAN WHO MADE IT ALL POSSIBLE

"If every state would join in Union Thanksgiving on
the 24th of this month, would it not be a renewed pledge of
love and loyalty to the Constitution of the United States,
which guarantees peace, prosperity, and perpetuity to
our great Republic?"

—The editorial written by Sarah Josepha Hale in
defense of Thanksgiving in *Godey's Lady's Book*,
1852

IN 1863 PRESIDENT Abraham Lincoln formally established a national holiday of Thanksgiving, designating
the last Thursday of November as the day. Thus,
Thanksgiving did not become a national holiday until
the darkest days of the Civil War.

One remarkable individual, Sarah Josepha Hale,
was the motivating force behind the acceptance of
Thanksgiving as a national holiday. Born in Newport,
New Hampshire, in 1788 and raised at a time when few women were formally educated, she became a woman of letters with a bent for creative
crusading. She was a household name for decades, but did not become a
public figure until she was 40—widowed, penniless, and the mother of five.

Her biographer, Ruth E. Finley, wrote that Mrs. Hale could weep copiously over a faded violet but also drive a sharp business deal. Her novels were popular at the time, and one of her nursery rhymes is still a hit. Sarah Hale wrote "Mary's Lamb," which we know as "Mary Had a Little Lamb." She wrote 36 books including ones that strongly advocated the abolition of slavery and the advancement of women. Her *Women's Record*, published in 1853, contained more than 1,500 biographical sketches of famous women.

She was one of the first American editors to pay her writers for their work, commissioning the likes of Hawthorne, Longfellow, Whittier, and Emerson.

As an editor of *Ladies Magazine* in Boston from 1828 to 1836 and then, beginning in 1837, as literary editor of *Godey's Lady's Book*, the foremost women's magazine in America in the 19th century, she conducted a long, personal campaign to establish a national Thanksgiving holiday. *Godey's* was based in Philadelphia, where Hale indignantly discovered, after moving there, that Thanksgiving was not observed here as it was in New England. Before 1863, Thanksgiving was primarily celebrated in New England and the West. Hale's efforts were redoubled.

She wrote to several presidents and many governors advocating her cause. She wrote hundreds of letters and once admitted to her readers, "My pen is weary from writing to these men. They pay little heed to my wishes. I shall continue to write them until they truly appreciate the fact Americans want this day of Thanksgiving."

This policy and program were consistently followed by her until 1863 when she succeeded in her purpose. Every November during these years a Thanksgiving editorial appeared in *Godey's*.

The editorial written by Mrs. Hale in defense of Thanksgiving in 1852 contained these lines: "Thanksgiving Day is a festival of ancient date in New England, being established there soon after the settlement of Boston. The observance has been gradually extending; and, for a few years past, efforts have been made to have a fixed day, which shall be universally observed throughout our whole country." The *Lady's Book* was the pioneer in this endeavor to give unity to the idea of Thanksgiving Day, and thus make it a national observance.

She continued: "The last Thursday in November was selected as the day, on the whole, most appropriate. Last year, twenty-nine [of 31] States, and all the Territories, united in the festival. This year, we trust that Virginia and Vermont will come into this arrangement, and that the Governor of each and all the States and Territories will appoint *Thursday, the 25th of November, as the Day of Thanksgiving.*"

In 1863, her final appeal—the one that would finally convince Lincoln—appeared in *Godey's.* It said in part:

"Would it not be a great advantage, socially, nationally, religiously, to have the day of our American Thanksgiving positively settled? Putting aside the sectional feelings and local incidents that might be urged by any single State or isolated Territory that desired to choose its own time, would it not be more noble, more truly American, to become national in unity when we offer to God our tribute of joy and gratitude for the blessings of the year?"

These editorials were supplemented by her personal letters written to Presidents Fillmore, Pierce, Buchanan, and Lincoln, as they entered office.

They were written with a constancy, consistent with her determined conviction, reinforced by personal letters and success with individual governors. Finally, public sentiment became so strong that the campaign needed only a great event to swing the balance in favor of her attitude. That event was the victory of the Union Army at the Battle of Gettysburg. Following Gettysburg, Lincoln recommended "that we invoke the influence of the Holy Spirit to subdue the anger that produced the strife."

The evidence of the part that Mrs. Hale played in having Thanksgiving revived as a national annual observance authorized by a Presidential Proclamation is to be found in an 1863 issue of the *Lady's Book*, when she wrote, "President Lincoln recognized the truth of these ideas (the unifying influence of a National day of thanks) as soon as they were presented to him. His reply to our appeal was a proclamation appointing, on October 3rd, the last Thursday in November 1863, as a day of National Thanksgiving."

Hale believed that the best time for Thanksgiving was the last Thursday in November, since "the agricultural labors of the year are generally completed." Idealistically, Hale saw Thanksgiving as a way to forestall the split between North and South, and, once that day had passed, as a way of healing the regional wounds after the war.

But there was more. She saw the holiday as a time for charitable giving, gratitude to God and advancement of the cause of peace. "Speak to your spouses," she urged her women readers, "and be not afraid to let them know your feelings on this matter. If they are just in their judgment, they will most certainly write to the men they have elected to political power, and persuade them to allow this day of prayer and thanksgiving."

In addition to all of this, it seemed that almost everything else she attempted seemed to turn out well, and her influence on American culture was vast.

Hale worked tirelessly on national monuments and symbols, spearheaded the movement to complete Boston's Bunker Hill Monument, and staged a monumental fair to raise the money needed. Before the Washington Monument was built, Bunker Hill was *the* American obelisk and first publicized tourist attraction. Hale also worked to make Mount Vernon a national shrine.

She crusaded for equal educational opportunities for women and was outspoken in her opposition to child labor. She founded the Seaman's Aid Society, the Ladies' Missionary Society of Philadelphia. She was the first American to speak against child labor and told her readers that America's poor needed jobs, not charity.

When she campaigned for women doctors, a masculine objector said, "You will drive men out of the medical profession and even those now in it will starve." To which she retorted: "If men cannot cope with women in the medical profession, let them take a humble occupation in which they can!"

She dared the powerful A. T. Stewart, founder of the New York department store, to cast convention to the winds and hire women clerks. He did, amid shouts from the clergy, who predicted that such a store would become a brothel. She was a pioneer in advocating that women should not only be allowed to have jobs but to control their own finances—a totally radical thought for the times.

For all of her big battles, she was not a stranger to smaller crusades. She had a strong aversion to the term "female," then applied to all women. She did not mince words in her 11-year fight against the term and ridiculed the word by referring to men as "males," printing such statements as: "A middle-aged male was found wandering the streets of Philadelphia in a dazed condition."

The battle reached its climax with her friend Matthew Vassar. She had encouraged this man to found the first college for women in this country, advised him to hire women teachers, helped devise the curriculum. Therefore, in 1861, she was stunned to discover that he had named this magnificent new venture Vassar Female College. Indignantly she wrote him: "What female do you mean? A female donkey?"

Finally, in 1866, Mr. Vassar gave in: "I hasten to inform you that the great agony is over."

Ever since the name has been Vassar College.

> "Take heart! Give thanks! To see clearly about us is to rejoice; and to rejoice is to worship the Father; and to worship Him is to receive more blessings still."
>
> —From Richard Nixon's 1972 Thanksgiving proclamation

GRACES AND BLESSINGS

"Earth with her thousand voices praises God."

—Samuel Taylor Coleridge

SAYING GRACE IS a custom of deepest charm and especially apropos at Thanksgiving.

Here, then, is a collection of graces and blessings that can be uttered:

The Book of Common Prayer is a basic source for many:

The Protestant

"Almighty God, Father of all mercies, we, thine unworthy servants, do give thee most humble and hearty thanks for all the goodness and loving-kindness to us, and to all men."

—*The Book of Common Prayer* (The Litany), 1662

For a Thanksgiving Service or Dinner

"We yield thee unfeigned thanks and praise, as for all thy mercies, so especially for the returns of seed-time and harvest, and for crowning the year with thy goodness in the increase of the ground, and the gathering in of the fruits thereof."

—Thanksgiving, *Book of Common Prayer*

"We give thee humble and hearty thanks for this thy bounty: beseeching thee to continue thy loving kindness to us; that our land may still yield her increase, to thy glory and our comfort."

—Collect for Thanksgiving Day, *Book of Common Prayer*

The Cowboy Grace

"Bless this food and us that eats it."

One of the appealing things about the Cowboy Grace, presumably from the Old West, is its complete homeliness; it is the one kind of prayer that allows humor to creep in.

The Danny Thomas Grace

> "For the air we breathe,
> and the water we drink,
> For a soul and a mind
> with which to think,
> For food that comes
> from fertile sod,
> For these, and many things,
> I'm thankful to my God."

—Thanksgiving grace written by comedian Danny Thomas
when he was in the sixth grade

Iowa Grace

"This is Thanksgiving Day—one of the best days of all the year. It has a mission all its own and blessing all its own to bestow upon all who open their souls to its beauty and good cheer. It should not be wholly given up to turkey and cranberry sauce. To eat, drink and be merry is a good way to give thanks—better than long prayers rendered with long faces, but it is not all that one ought to do today. A kind word kindly spoken to some one in distress; a worthy gift worthily bestowed upon some one more unfortunate—these are thanks acceptable on earth and in Heaven alike. . . . There is no man or woman so humble that their thanks to you for a gift bestowed to-day is not an incense that will rise to Heaven."

—Editorial November 27, 1890, in the *Iowa State Register*,
   proving that if the words are right it does not have to be
   created as a grace to serve as one

Emerson's "We Thank Thee"

> "For flowers that bloom about our feet;
> For tender grass, so fresh, so sweet;
> For song of bird, and hum of bee;
> For all things fair we hear or see,
>   Father in heaven, we thank Thee!
> For blue of stream and blue of sky;
> For pleasant shade of branches high;
> For fragrant air and cooling breeze,
> For beauty of the blooming trees,
>   Father in heaven, we thank Thee!"

—Ralph Waldo Emerson, used by some families as a special
   Thanksgiving grace

English Grace

"For what we are about to receive the Lord make us truly thankful, for Christ's sake. Amen."

Exclusionary Thanks

"O Lord, We thank Thee for the abundance and safe in-gathering of all our harvest except for a few fields between here and Stonehaven. . . ."   —Old English

The fact that such parody existed at all suggests to us how very common the custom of grace must have always been.

Facetious Grace

"Yes ma'am, no ma'am,
Thank you ma'am, please.
Open up the turkey's butt
And fork out the peas."

—Parody Thanksgiving grace, recalled in
Hennig Cohen and Tristram Peter Coffin,
The Folklore of American Holidays, 1987

Parody graces are common and used to shock one's elders. A Catholic man told me of a grace that he and his brothers love to give that went like this:

"Father, Son and Holy Ghost,
Whoever eats the fastest gets the most."

This always brought comments along the lines of, "We send him to parochial school and get this?"

The Furse Grace

"Give me a good digestion, Lord,
And also something to digest;
Give me a healthy body, Lord,

> And sense to keep it at its
> best."
>
> —Dr. Furse, Bishop of St. Albans

Grace Before Turkey

> "For turkey braised, the Lord be praised."
>
> —19th-century guide to turkey
>   preparation

Grace from Shakespeare

> "Let never day nor night unhallow'd pass,
> But still remember what the Lord hath done."
>
> —*2 Henry VI*, ii. 1. 85–86 *Henry VI, Part II*

The Hayes Grace

"The completed circle of summer and winter, seed-time and harvest, has brought us to the accustomed season at which a religious people celebrates with praise and thanksgiving the enduring mercy of Almighty God."

—From Rutherford B. Hayes's first Thanksgiving proclamation

The Honolulu Grace

"Lord, behold our family here assembled. We thank Thee for this place in which we dwell; for the love that unites us; for the peace accorded us this day; for the hope which we expect the morrow; for the health, the work, the food, and the bright skies, that make our lives delightful; for our friends in all parts of the earth.

"Give us courage and gaiety and the quiet mind. Spare to us our friends, soften to us our enemies. Bless us, if it may be, in all our innocent endeavors. If it may not, give us the strength to encounter that which is to come, that we be brave in peril, constant in tribulation, temperate in wrath, and in all changes of fortune, loyal and loving one to another.

"As the clay to the potter, as the windmill to the wind, as children of their sire, we beseech of Thee this help and mercy for Christ's sake."

—Robert Louis Stevenson, Thanksgiving Prayer,
delivered Thanksgiving Day, Honolulu, 1887

Humble Graces

"Thank the Lord for what we've getten,
If ther 'ad been mooar, mooar we shud hev
etten."

"For Thou'st placed upon the table, we thank the Lord, as weel's we're able."

"O thou that blest the loaves and fishes,
Look down upon these two poor dishes,

And tho' the murphies are but small,
O make them large enough for all,
For if they do our bellies fill
I'm sure it is a miracle."

Modern Grace

"It's Thanksgiving. Let's all microfilm our troubles and Xerox our blessings."

—Bob Orben, from *2100 Laughs for All Occasions*

The Newhart Grace

"For the food we are about to eat, please protect us."

—Bob Newhart, from the "Bob Newhart Show" after he has been presented with a roasted turkey from the brothers Darryl

Old Farm Grace

"Father in Heaven, we thank thee for our good beasts, which are dear to us next our kin. And on this Thanksgiving day, we ask Thy fond blessing upon them, for they cannot ask themselves. Amen."

Midland Graces

An article in the Omaha *World Herald* just before Thanksgiving in 1994 suggested that these two graces would commonly be heard in the Midlands these days.

"Bless these Thy gifts, most gracious
   God,
From whom all goodness springs;
Make clean our hearts and feed our
   souls
With good and joyful things."

—Traditional Christian grace

"Thank you for the wind and rain
   and sun and pleasant weather,
thank you for this our food
   and that we are together."

—Mennonite blessing

Refrain

"Lord of all to Thee we raise
This, our hymn of grateful praise!"

—The refrain of an old hymn of thanksgiving

A Scotch Grace

"Praise to God who giveth meat,
Convenient unto all to eat;
Praise for tea and buttered toast,
Father, Son and Holy Ghost."

The Selkirk Grace

"Some have meat but cannot eat;
Some could eat but have no meat;
We have meat and can all eat;
Blest, therefore, be God for our meat."

—Found in the papers of Dr. Plume of Maldon, Essex,
in a handwriting of about 1650

Another version, attributed to Robert Burns:

> "Some hae meat, and canna eat,
>   And some wad eat that want it;
> But we hae meat, and we can eat,
>   And sae the Lord be thankit."

A Thanksgiving Litany

> "For the abundance of the earth,
>   Dear Lord, we thank Thee.
> For this, the blessed land of our birth,
>   Dear Lord, we thank Thee.
> For heritage of pioneers;
> For freedom from all wants and fears,
> For strength and courage through the years,
>   Dear Lord, we thank Thee."

Traditional Jewish Blessing of the Bread

> *Praised are You, O Lord, our God, King of the universe Who brings forth bread from the earth.*

After this prayer is recited a piece of bread is sliced or broken from the loaf and passed around the table. Here is the same prayer transliterated from the Hebrew:

> *Barukh ala Adonai Eloheinu melekh haolam ha-motzi lehem min ha-aretz.*

Wartime Grace (1944)

> "Thanks for a lean board,
>   For scant harvest won!
> (Afar in the bleak lands
>   Our brothers have none.)
>
> "Thanks for the thin bread
>   Which answers our need.

(We make our feast frugal
That starved men may
feed.)

"Thanks for a stern faith
In seed-time and soil.
(Thousands die bravely
Defending our toil.)

"Thanks, under this flag,
For what we have not!
(With shares we now forfeit
Our freedom is bought.)"

—Edna Ewert, New Mexico, quoted in *This Is America*,
National Thanksgiving Association, under the
title "Grace Before Meat"

More to the point as a grace during war is this grace from Field Marshal Montgomery, which he uttered in 1943 and which was widely quoted:

"We must not forget to give thanks to the Lord, 'mighty in battle,' for giving us such a good beginning towards the attainment of our object. . . .

"And now let us get on with the job. Together with our American Allies, we have knocked Mussolini off his perch. We will now drive the Germans from Sicily."

Wessex Prayer

There is even a downright ungracious grace. This is one of the oldest that has survived. It was presumably said both at bedtime and at mealtime, but it is hard to imagine who would be so ungracious to utter this prayer:

> "God bless me and me wife,
> Me son John and his wife—
> Us four.
> No more."

The Winkworth Grace

> "Now thank we all our God,
> With heart and hand and voices
> Who wondrous things hath
>   done,
> In whom His world rejoices."
> —Catherine Winkworth: Tr. of Johann Crüger:
> Nun danket alle Gott, 1648

Wythorne Grace

It is natural to wonder what grace the Pilgrims might have used. Dr. Carleton Smith, chief of the Music Division, New York Public Library, was quoted in *This Week* magazine in November 1957 to the effect that one cannot be sure, but a grace that the Pilgrims likely used was one written by Thomas Wythorne:

"O Lord above, send us thy grace to be our stay,
 So as we never do that which brings unto the wicked sinful way,
 God bless the master of this house,
 God bless the mistress too;
 And all the little children
 Who round the table go."

Another typical grace of the same era incorporated other themes:

"O Lord our God and heavenly Father, which of thy unspeakable mercy towards us, hast provided meate and drinke for the nourishment of our weake bodies. Grant us peace to use them reverently, as from thy hands, with thankful hearts: let thy blessing rest upon these thy good creatures, to our comfort and sustenation: and grant wee humble beseech thee, good Lord, that as we doe hunger and thirst for this food of our bodies, so our soules may earnestly long after the food of eternall life, through Jesus Christ our Lord and Saviour, Amen."

Yvonne's Grace

"Bless, O Lord
These delectable vittles,
May they add to thy glory
And not to our middles."

—Yvonne Wright quoted as a "Thanksgiving Prayer"
in the 1986 *Reader's Digest Calendar*

Bready Forest Grace

A well-known Boston surgeon is fond of telling about how dreams of the "Bready Forest" may quite possibly have saved him from a life of skepticism. "When I was very little," he says, "I learned our family grace, which went: 'Thank Thee, dear Lord, for the love in our hearts and the Bready Forest.' Or at least, that's how I thought it went, and I always had such happy visions of the Bready Forest, a beautiful wonderland of all God's bounty where the food of man hung off the trees for the picking.

"I must have been ten or twelve before I discovered that the words really went: 'Thank Thee, dear Lord, for the love in our hearts and the bread before us.' But I wasn't a bit dismayed, because I knew that my Bready Forest was just what it meant all along."

Toasts for the Day

"Coming at the beginning of the farmer's rest, when the harvest is all gathered, this is a very joyous festival, and more than any other abounds in family reunions. Any toast therefore is appropriate which tells of the harvest, of fertility, of the closing year, of the family pride and traditions, of pleasure to young and old. At dinner, turkey and mince or pumpkin pie will of course be served, and these national favorites must not be forgotten by the toast-maker."

—Advice from the *Toaster's Handbook*, 1901

TWO VERBAL RITUALS are keys to the celebration of Thanksgiving. One is the grace spoken before dinner, and the second is the toast or toasts that are offered before drinking.

Toasting is an old custom of the Day, tied originally to the old Harvest Home celebrations when toasts were drunk to the lord and lady of the manor, such as the one that began:

"Here's a health to our master,
The lord of the feast,

> God bless his endeavors
> And send him increase."

Here is a small collection of American Thanksgiving toasts. If they sound quaint and old-fashioned, they should: most of these were well known by the turn of the century.

Toasts to the Day

> "For every day of life we're living,
>   Thanksgiving!
> For friends assembled 'round this board,
>   Thanks we're giving.
> For riches added to each hoard,
>   Thanks we're giving.
> For every blessing, great and small,
>   Thanks give we all!"
>
> —Ida E.S. Noyes

> "To Full Stomachs and Merry Hearts."

"The Great American Birds—May we have them where we love them best—the Turkeys on our tables, the Eagles in our pockets."

"Here are sincere wishes
  for whatever
will contribute most to your
  Thanksgiving joy
and happiness."

"Here's to the blessings of the year,
Here's to the friends we hold so dear,
To peace on earth, both far and near."

"Here's to the day when the Yankees first acknowledged Heaven's good gifts with Thank'ees."

"May our pleasures be boundless
while we have time to enjoy them."

"Thanksgiving—The magnetic festival that draws back erratic wanderers to the Old Folks at Home."

"Thanks to the Lord for the good things we eat,
Thanks to the Lord for the home where we
    meet,
  For our parents and wives
  And the loves of our lives
And the sweetest of sweethearts all sweet."

"The Thanksgiving Board—While it groans with plenty within, who cares for the whistling of the wind without?"

"Thanksgiving Day! Thanksgiving Day!
'Tis then our nation tries to pay
  Its heavy debt of gratitude
  For bountiful supplies of food,

> And richest blessings that expand
> To cover all of Freedom's land."

> "Ah! on Thanksgiving day, when from East and
>   from West,
> From North and South, come the Pilgrim and guest,
> When the gray-haired New Englander sees round his
>   board,
> The old broken links of affection restored,
> When the care-wearied man seeks his mother once
>   more,
> And the worn matron smiles where the girl smiled
>   before—
> What moistens the lips and what brightens the eye,
> What calls back the past, like the rich pumpkin pie?"

"To the pastimes of Thanksgiving and the present times in which we enjoy them."

"To our national birds—
  The American Eagle,
  The Thanksgiving Turkey:
  May one give us peace in all our States—
  And the other a piece for all our plates."

—A very popular and common Thanksgiving toast of the 19th and early 20th century, there were a number of variations on this toast including this one:

"The Two National Fowls of America—The Federal Eagle and the Festal Turkey. May we always have peace under the wings of the one, and be able to obtain a piece from the breast of the other."

And this one (with clear "best government is the least government" overtones):

"The Turkey and the Eagle—We love to have the one soar high, but wish the other to roost low."

"Thrice welcome the day in its annual round;
  What treasures of love in its bosom are found;
  New England's high holiday, ancient and dear,
  'Twould be twice as welcome if twice in a year."

"To the inventor of pumpkin pie—God bless her."

(This toast echoes its times assuming all things culinary are female, so one may wish to amend it to say him/her. Then again, one may not.)

> "When turkey's on the table laid,
>   And good things I may scan,
> I'm thankful that I wasn't made
>   A vegetarian."

—Edgar A. Guest

Toasts to the Bird

Time was when the turkey was toasted before the carving began as part of the ritual of the meal. Commonly, a line from classical literature was used. Anyone wishing to revive the custom can pick from this collection.

> "Nothing in his life
> Became him like the leaving it."

—Shakespeare, *Macbeth*, i. 4. 7–8

"Appoint a meeting with this old fat fellow."

—Shakespeare, *The Merry Wives of Windsor,* iv. 4. 15

"He made me mad
To see him shine so brisk and smell so sweet."

—Shakespeare, *1 Henry IV,* i. 3. 53–54

"Here he comes, swelling like a turkey-cock."

—Shakespeare, *Henry V,* v. 1. 15

"Stuffed with all honourable virtues."

—Shakespeare, *Much Ado About
Nothing,* i. 1. 56

"Let the land
Look for his peer:
he has not yet been
found."

—Thomas B. Aldrich

"Is this that haughty gallant, gay Lothario?"

—Nicholas Rowe, *Fair Penitent*, v. 1

Toasting Tip for Sippers

There was a time when it was customary to issue a volley of toasts, mixed willy-nilly. The first round might have sounded something like this: *"To The Inventor of Pumpkin Pie—to Peace with all Nations—to The Rulers of our Country—to The Farmer—to Full Stomachs and Merry Hearts—to their Excellencies, the President and the Governor; may we obey all their commands as willingly as when they tell us to feast—Abounding Plenty; may we always remember the Source from which our benefits come."*

Well and good, but not for gulpers.

"I guess I'll have another beer."

—Marine private, Hue, South Vietnam, asked about his special plans for Thanksgiving, November 22, 1972

MENUS FROM THANKSGIVINGS PAST

"When ye have gathered in the fruit of the land, ye shall keep
a feast unto the Lord."

—Leviticus 23:39

"Shining red apples and clusters of grapes,
Nuts and a host of good things,
Chickens and turkeys and fat little pigs,—
These are what Thanksgiving brings."

—Traditional

HERE, IN CHRONOLOGICAL order, are Thanksgiving menus to bring a sparkle
to the eye and a rumble to the stomach.

1621

There is no exact record of the bill of fare for the famous harvest festival of 1621, which is now known as the "first Thanksgiving." The event is mentioned only in two quotes, one from William Bradford's *Of Plimoth Plantation* and the other in a letter of Edward Winslow's included in *Mourt's Relation*. From those sources and by making other assumptions the staff of Plimoth Plantation, where much research is conducted on the original settlement, have come up with the following menu with those marked with an asterisk presumed to have been present:

> Boiled codfish*
> Grilled seabass and other fish*
> Roast fowl* (including ducks, geese, swans, and "a great
> store of wild turkeys") with "pudding in the belly"
> (stuffing)
> Corn meal
> Roast venison* (the meat of five deer brought by
> Indians) with sausage
> Bread of Indian corn
> "Compound Sallet" (mixed vegetables, perhaps beans,
> pumpkin, and squash)
> Boiled onions
> Crab apples and currants
> Chestnuts, hickory nuts

Bag pudding

Beer, Aqua Vitae (strong spirits), water

1769

Forefather's Day, Plymouth, was when much of the early linking of the Pilgrims and Thanksgiving took place. Here is the menu from an early Plymouth gathering:

1. A large baked Indian whortleberry pudding.
2. A dish of sauquetach [succotash].
3. A dish of clams.
4. A dish of oysters and a dish of cod-fish.
5. A haunch of venison, roasted by the first jack [or spit] brought to the colony.
6. A dish of sea-fowl.
7. A dish of frost-fish and eels.
8. An apple pie.
9. A course of cranberry tarts and cheese made in the Old Colony.

1870

In 1870, a Des Moines editor printed the Thanksgiving menu of the Savery House. After observing that it was not customary to print such menus, he reminded readers that the "high reputation" of the Savery House was so "universally known" that nothing could be said to add to its reputation. It appeared in print as follows:

SOUP—Oyster

FISH—Mackinaw Trout, with fine herb sauce

BOILED—Tongue; Ham; Leg of Mutton; Corned Beef; Turkey, with oyster sauce; Chicken, with Marrinaise sauce

ROAST—Prairie chicken, with currant jelly; Turkey with giblet sauce; Veal, with dressing; Ribs of Beef; Sirloin of Beef; Mutton; Lamb; Saddle of Venison, with cranberry jelly; Sirloin of Buffalo; Goose, with apple sauce; Mallard Duck a la Creole

COLD—Corned Beef; Tongue; Mutton; Chicken Salad; Lobster Salad

ENTREE—Broiled Quail, with toast; Buffalo Steak, a la Maitre d'Hotel; Braized Teal Duck, with olives; Wild Goose, a la Regent; Pork and Beans, baked Boston style; Fillets of Chicken, a l'Anglaise; Belle Fritters, vanilla flavor; Haricot of Venison, with pastry

VEGETABLES OF THE SEASON

RELISHES—Pickled Beets; Worcestershire Sauce; Pepper Sauce; Chow Chow; French Mustard; Sliced Tomatoes; Tomato Catsup; Boston Pickles; Cheese; Walnut Catsup

PASTRY—Mince Pie; Old Style Yankee Pumpkin Pie; Steamed Apple Pudding; Lemon Sauce

DESSERT—Pound Cake; Sponge Cake; Swedish Pound Cake; French Cream Cake; Jelly Cake; Jumbles; Rum Jelly; Doughnuts; Blancmange; German Meranges; Kisses; English Walnuts; Filberts; Almonds; Raisins; Apples

TEA AND COFFEES

WINES—From the Savery House cellars

1887

In many families, Thanksgiving now entailed interspersing the old-fashioned chicken pie turkey and mashed turnips with more elegant dishes and serving them in the new, "correct" order, as suggested by the following 1887 menu from the *Woman's Home Companion*. It is interesting to note that turkey is on this bill of fare and was missing from the previous one. It was always a staple of a New England Thanksgiving, but took a while to catch on elsewhere. Prior to the Civil War chicken pie was probably as popular as turkey and some places more so. There have always been regional differences in the way the meal is staged—for instance, for generations the people of Baltimore have deemed sauerkraut an important element of the feast.

DINNER

Raw Oysters   Turtle Soup
Boiled Fish, with Anchovy Sauce
Roast Turkey, Giblet Sauce
Smothered Guinea Fowl   Chicken Pie
Roast Haunch of Venison
Mashed Potatoes   Sweet Potatoes
Mashed Turnips
Cauliflower   Boiled Onions
Baked Salsify   Cabbage Salad

Cranberry Sauce   Celery
Sweet Peach Pickle
Pumpkin Pie   Mince Pie
Thanksgiving Pudding
Ice Cream   Thanksgiving Cake
Crackers   Cheese   Pickles
Fruit   Oranges
Grapes

1890

It is the family dinner following church services that most nearly typifies Thanksgiving. In 1890 we find the following from *Harper's Bazaar*:

"Soup, fish, salad, and *entrees* may be appropriate and elegant on 364 days in the year, but on the 365th let them be banished, and let the traditional turkey and his vegetable satellites, the toothsome chicken pie, and all the triumphs of the Yankee housewife, reign supreme. Let that national holiday be kept with national dishes, and let there be a joyful and honourable pride in them, with never a tinge of shame that their palatableness is not hidden behind French names."

1891

In 1891, while the McKinleys dined simply on turkey and potatoes presented by an Idaho friend, Mr. E.K. Sanborn, the manager of a local hostelry, supplied the following menus which he "thinks is ideal from the standpoint of an American." Here goes: "Lynn Haven oysters, olives, celery, caviar, Johannis burger Schloss 1865, green turtle soup, sherry, dry Soleras 1870, potato croquettes, Chesapeake diamondback terrapin, Saratoga potatoes, saddle of venison, currant jelly, Madeira, Amory Dom Pedro 1791–1792; orange Romaine salad, roast turkey stuffed with truffles, cranberry sauce, French baked potatoes, boiled onions, stuffed green peppers, champagne, vintage 1894; tomato and artichoke salade, mince pie, cheese, nuts, raisins, liqueurs."

1900

Some well-to-do families, however, became so carried away by the urge to imitate French haute cuisine that they abandoned American tradition completely. This menu, suggested by *Harper's Bazaar* in 1900, retains roast turkey alone of all the traditional dishes; even cranberry sauce is omitted. It almost makes Thanksgiving sound like a French tradition beginning with the oysters and calling stuffed olives "olives farcies."

MENU FOR TWELVE COVERS

Huîtres

Buzzard Bay.

Soup

Purée of game.

Hors-d'oeuvre

Olives farcies.   Salted almonds.
Canapés of caviare.
Canapés with anchovy sauce.

Fish

Lobster in shells, garnished with oyster crabs.
Potato croquettes with cheese.

Entrées

Small timbales, Bretonne.
Filet of venison with artichokes.
Jellied pâté of goose livers with truffles.
Romaine salad.

Roast

Turkey decorated with glazed chestnuts.

Dessert

Thanksgiving monument of ice-cream.
Cakes.
Camembert cheese.
Coffee.

1937

Before the Second World War, the President's Thanksgiving dinner was news. Here is an Associated Press dispatch from 1937:

WASHINGTON, Nov. 24.—The menu for President Roosevelt's Thanksgiving dinner:

Oyster cocktail, saltines.

Clear soup with sherry, curled celery, toast fingers, olives.

Roast turkey, chestnut dressing, cranberry jelly, Deerfoot sausages.

String beans, scalloped sweet potatoes and apples.

Grapefruit and orange salad, cheese straws.

Pumpkin pie, ice cream, coffee.

> "We forget to appreciate the simplicity of Thanksgiving.
> Psychologically it's probably the least complicated holiday we
> celebrate and the only one that is secularly religious.
> Thanksgiving is not owned by just one religion. It's an
> American holiday. Since the holiday is acknowledged by nearly
> everyone, it's one of the few holidays couples of mixed
> religious backgrounds can celebrate together without risking
> conflict."
>
> —Peter Cimbolic, Catholic University, *Washington Post*,
> November 18, 1988

READYING THE FEAST AND PREPARING A FEW TRIMMINGS AND DESSERTS

"This Thanksgiving festival was always kept at Plumfield in the good old-fashioned way, and nothing was allowed to interfere with it. For days beforehand, the little girls helped Asia and Mrs. Jo in storeroom and kitchen, making pies and puddings, sorting fruit, dusting dishes, and being very busy and immensely important. The boys hovered on the outskirts of the forbidden ground, sniffing the savory odors, peeping in at the mysterious performances, and occasionally being permitted to taste some delicacy in the process of preparation."

—From *Little Men*, by Louisa May Alcott (1832–1888)

WHEN IT COMES to coping with Thanksgiving, there's nothing like a battle plan. Everything gets busier and busier, as one gets closer to the Day and planning gets more and more important.

"In the ideal Thanksgiving dinner," wrote Teresa Gibbons, United Press Syndicate, for Thanksgiving 1994, "the Norman Rockwell Thanksgiving meal, the cook starts weeks ahead of time, polishing silver, chopping cranberries and making corn bread for homemade stuffing.

"The days leading up to the holiday meal are a glorious countdown of pureeing pumpkin and rolling pie crusts, of roasting chestnuts and brewing cider. When the family gathers around the table, the meal is a stunning production that shows the hours of time and energy the cook has devoted.

"Welcome to the real world, where folks work or simply don't have the time to give Thursday's Thanksgiving dinner a thought until Wednesday."

Here are things to consider:

—Thawing. If you use a frozen turkey, thaw it in the refrigerator, allowing one day for every five pounds. If you don't have the time, you can defrost the tightly wrapped turkey faster in cold water—changing the water every 30 minutes. Fresh or defrosted turkey will keep in the fridge for up to two days.

—Planning #1. People are usually hungry when they arrive. Plan on something like a small cup of soup to stave off hunger pangs and keep the horde from getting too grumpy while waiting for the meal.

—Planning #2. Cookbook author Nathalie Dupree has suggested: "When planning your Thanksgiving menu, ask guests if there's some dish they absolutely must have. Then suggest they bring it themselves. That way, they get their favorite and you don't leave yourself open to abuse for not preparing it the way their mom/grandma/spouse always does it."

—Planning #3. This may sound silly but one should check to make sure that the turkey and the roasting pan fit into your oven before you plan to cook it.

—Set up a table with a big jigsaw puzzle. It will give people something to do and will keep them out of your hair while you finish cooking.

While the turkey is thawing, you can begin readying the trimmings.

There will be dozens of recipes in the newspapers the week before Thanksgiving, but here are a few special examples.

Cranberry Trimmings

Cranberry Sauce/Relish

Whole berries are easy; just empty the bag into water and add a lot of sugar, but you don't have to. As one canny food editor put it a few Thanksgivings ago, "Canned was good enough for our parents, there's plenty frozen and besides, it is just a sauce. You don't make your own hot dog relish." Craig Claiborne is on record with the statement, "I can never approve of anybody taking cranberry sauce out of a can," but this is only something to consider if you are inviting Craig Claiborne to your house.

Fresh Cranberry Sauce

2 cups sugar
2 cups water
4 cups cranberries

Combine sugar and water. Cook together 5 minutes. Add cranberries. Cook without stirring until all the skins pop open, about 5 minutes. Remove from heat and allow sauce to remain in saucepan until cool. Makes 1 quart.

Nobody's Fool

2 cups cranberries
$\frac{1}{2}$ cup granulated sugar
$\frac{1}{2}$ cup brown sugar
Juice of 2 oranges
Grated rind of 1 orange
2 whole star anise
$1\frac{1}{2}$ cups whipping cream
Orange rind, mint springs for garnish

Combine all ingredients except cream and garnishes in a saucepan. Heat to a boil over medium heat, stirring now and then to prevent sticking. Reduce heat and simmer, uncovered, for 20 minutes. Remove anise. Refrigerate until cold or up to 1 week.

Whip the cream in a cold bowl with cold beaters, to stiff peaks.

To serve, fold $\frac{3}{4}$ cup of the chilled cranberry sauce, leaving streaks, into the whipped cream. Spoon into a stemmed serving dish. (The cranberry mixture should be folded into the cream just before serving to prevent weeping.)

Rosa Poliakoff's Furiously Stirred Whole Berry Cranberry Sauce

3 bags (12 oz. each) cranberries
4 cups sugar
½ cup water (scant)

Heat sugar and water, stirring constantly. Watch carefully; when mixture reaches jelly stage on a candy thermometer (220 degrees), add cranberries. Stir furiously; cook until cranberries pop. Chill. Drain before serving.

Notes: Use the drained syrup on fresh fruit or to poach pears.
It is better if the cranberries are fresh. The cranberries should be dry.

My notes: It's worth the trouble of once a year using the candy thermometer to make this delicious whole berry sauce. The sound of the berries as they cook and the wonderful rich color of the sauce make it worthwhile. And the cranberries, refrigerated, keep forever—after all, they're well preserved in sugar!

Rosa Poliakoff lives in Abbeville, South Carolina.

Cranberry Crunch

1 (16-ounce) can whole cranberry sauce
½ cup quick-cooking rolled oats
¼ cup all-purpose flour
½ cup brown sugar
4 tablespoons butter or margarine
Whipped cream or vanilla ice cream

Heat oven to 360°F. Spread cranberry sauce in 9-inch pie plate. Combine oats, flour and brown sugar; cut in butter until crumbly. Sprinkle over the cranberries. Bake for 25 minutes. Top with whipped cream or vanilla ice cream.

Makes 5 servings.

Susan Stamberg's Cranberry Relish
(from her book *Talk*)

"At the first Thanksgiving of my married life, in Allentown, Pennsylvania, my mother-in-law, Marjorie Stamberg, served a fabulous and fascinating cranberry relish. So fascinating that I asked for the recipe, which she kindly provided:

2 cups raw cranberries
1 small onion (that's the fascinating part)
½ cup sugar

¾ cup sour cream
2 tablespoons horseradish (that's the other fascinating part)

Procedure: Grind the cranberries and onion together. Add all the other ingredients and mix. Put in a plastic container and freeze. A few hours before serving, move the container from the freezer to the refrigerator to thaw. The relish will be thick, creamy, chunky, and shocking pink. Makes 1½ pints."

Other Trimmings

Long Island Corn Pudding

4 ears fresh corn
2 cups Half-and-Half
2 tablespoons cornstarch, sifted
3 eggs, well beaten
1 tablespoon granulated sugar
1 teaspoon salt
4 tablespoons butter, melted

1. Remove kernels and liquid residue from corn cobs. There should be about 2 cups. In a medium bowl, combine corn with liquid, Half-and-Half, cornstarch, eggs, sugar, salt and melted butter.

2. Stir until well combined. Pour mixture into a shallow, buttered, 1½-inch-deep baking dish. Bake in a 350° oven for 60 minutes or until a knife inserted in center comes out clean.

Berkeley Plantation Fried Sweet Potatoes

6 medium-sized sweet potatoes
2 cups flour
½ cup white sugar
2 teaspoons cinnamon
honey

Parboil sweet potatoes, peel and cut potatoes lengthwise into 1-inch strips. Roll in flour, white sugar and cinnamon. Drop in deep-fat fryer and brown until crisp.

Serve with honey for dipping.

Serves four people, 3 strips each.

Two Pies

Classic Pumpkin Pie

Choose the smaller spice amounts for gentle seasoning, golden color—more spice for robust flavor, deep color.

  1½ **cups canned or mashed cooked pumpkin**
  ¾ **cup sugar**
  ½ **teaspoon salt**
  1 **to 1¼ teaspoons cinnamon**
  ½ **to 1 teaspoon ginger**
  ¼ **to ½ teaspoon nutmeg**
  ¼ **to ½ teaspoon cloves**
  3 **slightly beaten eggs**
  1¼ **cups milk**
  1 **6-ounce can (⅔ cup) evaporated milk**
  1 **unbaked 9-inch pastry shell, edges crimped** *high*

Thoroughly mix pumpkin, sugar, salt, and spices. Blend in eggs, milk, and evaporated milk. Pour the filling into the unbaked pastry shell. (For no spills, do this on the oven rack.) Bake in a hot oven (400°) 50 minutes or till a knife inserted halfway between the center and the edge comes out clean. Cool before serving.

Mary McLeod Bethune's Sweet Potato Pie

Filling

9 medium sweet potatoes or yams (about 4 pounds)
1 cup (2 sticks) butter or margarine, softened
½ cup granulated sugar
½ cup firmly packed brown sugar
½ teaspoon salt
¼ teaspoon nutmeg
3 eggs, well beaten
2 cups milk
1 tablespoon vanilla

Crust

3 unbaked 9-inch Classic Crisco Single Crusts

Boil sweet potatoes until tender. Peel and mash.
Heat oven to 350° F.
Combine butter, granulated sugar, brown sugar, salt and nutmeg in large bowl. Beat at medium speed with electric mixer until creamy. Beat in sweet potatoes until well mixed. Beat in eggs. Beat in milk and vanilla slowly. Spoon into 3 unbaked pie shells, using about 4 cups filling per shell.

Bake at 350° for 50 to 60 minutes or until set. Cool to room temperature before serving. Store in refrigerator.

"I wish the bald eagle had not been chosen as the
representative of our country: he is a bird of bad moral
character ... he is generally poor, and often very lousy. The
turkey is a much more respectful bird and withal a true
original native of America."

—Benjamin Franklin (1784)

This quotation has long been used to say that Franklin actually lobbied to
make the turkey the national bird. Not so. He made the point in a letter to
his daughter in which he was reacting to the French who could not figure
out why the Americans had picked the eagle as their national bird because
it *looked too much like a turkey.*

THE STUFFING

"If roasting a turkey is a straightforward procedure, involving time, temperature and math, it is in the trimmings that cooks show the most artistry. Stuffing shows off creativity, gravy displays finesse, and side dishes reveal our penchant for sweets or nutrition . . ."

—Thanksgiving Food Section, *The St. Petersburg Times*, November 18, 1994

THIS MAY BE the best part of the meal, and it's as easy or hard as you want to make it. But it is essential. What would a traditional holiday dinner be without stuffing? Or, some call it dressing. Doesn't matter what you call it: the stuff just tastes good.

Bags of croutons come with ample instructions and seasoning. You can spice them up with sautéed onions and celery, cooked sausage and bacon, fresh mushrooms, herbs, walnuts, and more. Others have a sweet taste when apples, raisins, or other fruits are added.

On the other hand, you may want to work from scratch. Here are a few tips followed by eight top-notch stuffing recipes—two with White House pedigrees.

Stuffing Tips. Points and principles that may come in handy in the creation of stuffing:

- Each of us probably has a favorite type of stuffing. Most likely it's the stuffing your mother or grandmother made. In the North, stuffing is made with day-old bread, while Southerners make their stuffing with cornbread.
- In her *Way to Cook*, Julia Child says that stuffing should be room temperature when it is put into the turkey, so as not to throw off the timing of the roasting of the bird.
- Not all stuffings use bread as the main ingredient. Perhaps in your heritage is Cajun and Dirty Rice Dressing, made with rice, sausage and other seasonings.
- Stuffing tends to be forgiving so one should feel free to add or subtract with some freedom.
- Plan on about a cup of stuffing per pound of turkey.
- Use a fork to toss ingredients together to prevent the stuffing from becoming too compact.
- Microwave all vegetables, meat, and seafood before combining them with other stuffing ingredients.
- Don't stuff the turkey until just before it goes in the oven.
- Some think you should cook stuffing in a separate container (check directions for adding extra liquid), not in the turkey. Some advocate heating stuffing in a microwave-to-table dish rather than stuffing a big bird. This way you can start the turkey before making the stuffing.

You'll have plenty of time to make the stuffing and the bird will cook faster. Others believe the only way to cook stuffing is in the bird.

• Moisten stuffing with vegetable or poultry broth in lieu of eggs to save calories and cholesterol.

Bill Hickman's
Southeast Texas Turkey Dressing

Cornbread mix, 3 small standard boxes
Bulk sausage (good quality), 2 pounds
Green onions, 1 large bunch sliced
Regular onions, 1 large chopped
Parsley, 1 bunch chopped
Pecans, 1 cup
Raisins, 1 cup
Granny Smith apples, 2 cored and chopped
Black pepper, to taste
Chicken broth, 2 or 3 cans

Make cornbread according to instructions on boxes; crumble and cook sausage, reserving about one tablespoon of grease; sauté green and regular onions in reserved grease; add all ingredients, including enough broth for desired moisture. Use as stuffing in the bird or heat in a separate covered pan or casserole. Enjoy, y'all.

Chestnut Stuffing

2 pounds fresh chestnuts or 3 (8-ounce) jars vacuum-packed roasted whole chestnuts
1 cup unsalted butter, divided
2 medium onions, peeled and chopped
1½ cups chopped celery with leaves
1½ tablespoons rubbed or ground sage
2 teaspoons dried thyme, crumbled
2 teaspoons pepper
2 (1-pound) loaves white bread, crusts trimmed and bread cut into cubes
Salt

To prepare fresh chestnuts: Cut an X on one side of each chestnut with sharp knife. Place nuts in large saucepan of simmering water and cook 12 minutes. Remove pan from heat. Remove one nut using slotted spoon. Grasp nut in dishtowel. Using sharp knife, peel off shell and dark inner skin. Repeat with remaining chestnuts.

Coarsely chop freshly prepared or vacuum-packed chestnuts. Can be made 1 week in advance. Wrap tightly and freeze. Thaw completely before using.

Melt ¼ cup (half stick) butter in large heavy skillet over medium heat. Add onions, celery, herbs and pepper and sauté until onions are tender, about 10 minutes. Place bread cubes in large bowl. Pour onion mixture over bread. Melt ¼ cup butter in same skillet over medium heat. Add chopped chestnuts and sauté until golden brown, about 8 minutes. Add to bread mixture. Melt remaining ½ cup butter in same skillet. Pour over bread mixture and toss well. Season with salt. Stuffing can be made 1 day ahead. Cover and refrigerate.

Makes enough to stuff 15-pound turkey.

Lemon Sage Dressing

½ cup butter or margarine
1 cup sliced celery
½ cup sliced green onions
½ cup shredded carrot
8 cups unseasoned stuffing cubes
½ teaspoon grated lemon peel
½ teaspoon dried sage leaves
½ teaspoon salt
⅛ teaspoon pepper
1½ cups canned chicken broth

Heat oven to 325° F.

Melt butter. Add celery, onions and carrot. Sauté until vegetables are tender. Stir in remaining ingredients.

Pour into 1½-quart casserole and bake 30 to 45 minutes.

Makes 8 servings.

Old-Fashioned Bread Stuffing

1½ cups chopped onion
1½ cups chopped celery
½ cup margarine or butter
1 teaspoon poultry seasoning
1 teaspoon rubbed sage
1 teaspoon salt
Dash ground black pepper
½ cup water or chicken broth
8 cups dried bread cubes (10–12 bread slices, cubed and dried overnight)

Cook and stir onion and celery in margarine in medium skillet over medium heat until tender. Stir in seasonings.

Add onion mixture and water to bread cubes in large bowl. Toss to mix. Makes 8 cups, enough for a 12- to 14-pound turkey.

—Source: Butterball Turkey Talk-Line

Lebanon, Pennsylvania, Stuffing

(For 18- to 20-lb. turkey)

Turkey neck, heart, gizzard, liver
2 qts. water
1 large loaf stale bread
½ bunch parsley
2 onions
10 stalks and tender leaves celery
⅓ lb. butter or butter substitute
1 egg (well beaten)
3 hard-cooked eggs
½ teaspoon poultry seasoning
Salt and pepper

Simmer neck, heart and gizzard in the water for about two hours, then add the liver and simmer about one hour longer or until meat may be easily scraped from the neck. Take out meat from the liquid and put it through food grinder, using large blade. (Set broth aside for use later.) Put onions, parsley (do not use large stems) and celery through the food chopper or chop fine in bowl. Chop the hard-cooked eggs. Cut bread in small squares. Melt butter (or margarine or cooking oil) in skillet, add bread squares, ground turkey meat and giblets, chopped parsley, onions and celery. Mix and heat thoroughly until the bread is well saturated with the hot fat. Add the well-beaten egg and mix in, then the chopped hard-cooked eggs, the seasonings and enough of the broth in which turkey bits were cooked to make dressing the consistency of potato salad. It should be moist but not wet. You will find that you need about 1½ cups of the broth for the dressing. The remainder of the broth may be used for gravy.

—New Hobby Horse Cookery

Cherry-Rice Stuffing

½ cup butter or margarine
3 cups diced celery with leaves
2 1-pound cans red sour pitted cherries (water pack)
2 10.5-ounce cans condensed chicken consomme
2 tsp. seasoned salt
2 tsp. grated orange rind
1 15-ounce box or 3.5-ounce boxes precooked rice

Melt butter in 3-quart saucepan. Add celery and cook over low heat until tender. Drain cherries; combine juice with chicken consomme and add enough water to make 4½ cups liquid; pour into saucepan with celery. Add seasoned salt and orange rind; bring to a boil. Add rice, cover tightly and let stand 13 minutes. Stir in cherries. Use as stuffing for turkey, or for 2 ducks or chickens.

(Makes stuffing for 12–14-lb. turkey)

Lady Bird Johnson's Turkey Dressing

1 medium-sized pan of corn bread
4 slices toasted white bread
1 stalk chopped celery
3 large onions, chopped
6 eggs
¼ cup butter
Salt
Pepper
Sage
Stock from turkey

Mix crumbled bread and corn bread with stock from turkey. Be sure to use enough stock so it will not be stiff. Add eggs and remaining ingredients. Bake slowly for one hour. Serves 8.

(As this recipe calls for stock from turkey, it presumes that (a) you cooked the turkey first, (b) froze stock from the previous turkey, or (c) substitute chicken stock.)

White House Oyster Dressing

François Rysavy, in his book *White House Chef*, detailed the oyster stuffing favored by President Dwight David Eisenhower.

For a 15- to 18-pound turkey.

"I clean the turkey, take out the insides and cook the neck, all the giblets except the liver in 6 cups water (to which I have added onion, 1 medium sliced; 3 stalks celery, 2 carrots, 1 clove garlic and 1½ teaspoons salt). Later I use the stock for stuffing.

"I grind 1½ loaves stale bread coarsely. Then I add to it the same amount of bulk as the bread made up of the following ingredients: 2 cups chopped celery, 2 cups chopped onions, and seasoning of 1 teaspoon salt and pepper to taste. I do not use sage or bay leaves which I think spoil the flavor of a turkey stuffing.

"The onion and celery are first gently softened in a stick and a half of butter before they are added to the bread.

"I use the meat from the neck and gizzard, chopped fine, I combine this with 2 quarts whole oysters which have been parboiled in their own juice until the edges curl; 1 cup either precooked or sautéed mushrooms, and finally, the liver of the turkey which has been fine-chopped raw. I add this to the bread mixture and additional seasoning if necessary. Now I add stock to make a rather dry stuffing, but if there is not enough liquid, I add sweet cream, which goes well with oysters. As a matter of fact, I try to make sure to add sweet cream by putting in ½ cup first before I finish with the stock.

"I rub 2 teaspoons salt and pepper to taste inside the turkey and stuff the turkey, sewing it shut."

Roanoke Pecan Stuffing

Turkey, capon or roasting chicken
4 cups water
2 stalks celery, washed
1 peeled carrot, cut into ½-inch slices
1 small onion, cut into quarters
1 cup butter or margarine
2 cups thinly sliced celery
2 cups chopped onions
½ cup finely chopped parsley
1 cup long grain rice
4 cups small corn bread pieces
2 cups small torn whole wheat bread pieces
2 cups chopped pecans
2 cans (4 oz. each) mushroom stems and pieces, undrained
3 teaspoons poultry seasoning
1½ teaspoons salt
½ teaspoon pepper

Combine turkey, capon or roasting chicken neck and gizzard, water, stalks of celery, carrot slices and onion quarters in saucepan; cover and simmer gently until gizzard is tender. Set aside to cool stock. Discard vegetables and neck piece. Cut gizzard into small pieces. Melt ½ cup butter or margarine in fry pan. Add sliced celery, chopped onion and parsley; cook over low heat until tender but not brown. Set aside. Brown unwashed rice in remaining ½ cup butter in fry pan or Dutch oven. Add poultry stock and enough water to make 3 cups liquid. Simmer 10 minutes, stirring constantly. Combine in large mixing bowl the breads, celery-onion mixture, rice and stock, pecans, mushrooms, seasonings; mix well. Season cavity of bird with salt; stuff loosely with dressing; skewer and roast poultry as desired. Yield: 12 cups stuffing or enough for a 12-pound bird. (One cup dressing for each pound is the general rule.)

German Stuffing With Sauerkraut
(Enough for a 10-pound turkey)

> 1 large onion, finely chopped
> 3 pounds sauerkraut, rinsed thoroughly and drained
> 3 juniper berries
> 1 tablespoon caraway seeds
> ½ cup dry white wine
> 1 large raw potato, peeled
> Salt and pepper to taste

Sauté apple and onion in butter until soft. Add well-drained sauerkraut, juniper berries, caraway, and cook over low heat for 8 to 10 minutes. Add wine; raise heat and simmer. Grate potato in food processor, blender or with hand grater. Add it bit by bit to sauerkraut mixture, stirring. Cook until mixture has thickened and becomes dry. Season with salt and pepper. Cool before stuffing bird.

A final note: Watch out for some of the old-fashioned recipes if you are trying to keep your diet under control. The Buffalo *News* occasionally repeats a recipe with the name "Dr. Billings' Turkey Stuffing." Here is the recipe and—no—the butter measurement is *not* a mistake.

2 large loaves, white bread, crusts removed
1 medium onion, chopped
Salt and pepper
1 or 2 teaspoons sage
1 pound butter

Crumble bread into a bowl. Add onion, salt, pepper and sage; mix well. Melt butter and pour gradually over the crumbs, tossing to distribute well. This recipe makes enough to stuff a 25-pound turkey.

"I painted the turkey in 'Freedom from Want' on Thanksgiving Day. Mrs. Wheaton, our cook (and the lady holding the turkey in the picture) cooked it, I painted it, and we ate it. That was one of the few times I've ever eaten the model."

—Norman Rockwell, on his famous painting of Thanksgiving dinner, from *My Adventures as an Illustrator*, 1960

USEFUL INFORMATION ON THE CULINARY
CUSTOMS AND RITUALS OF THE DAY

"I just yell at the bird and hope the meat will fall off."

—Jeff Smith, television's Frugal Gourmet,
who is not a carver

"Carving is a skill, like parallel parking or programming a VCR.
It takes practice."

—Karol V. Menzie, *The Baltimore Sun*

On Carving

FIRST SOME CONCEPTUAL advice from "The Perfect Gentleman," 1860:

"A great deal of the comfort and satisfaction of a good dinner depends upon the *carving*. Awkward carving is enough to spoil the appetite of a refined and sensitive person. No matter how well the meats may be cooked, if they are mutilated, torn, and hacked to pieces, or even cut awkwardly, one half of the relish is destroyed by the carver. Formerly, in England, there were regular teachers of the art of carving and Lady Mary Wortly Montague confesses that she once took lessons of such a professor three times a week. Besides the annoyance and mortification of bad carving, it is a very extravagant piece of ignorance, as it causes a great waste of meats. In the seventeenth century, carving was a science that carried with it as much pedantry as the business of school-teaching does at the present day; and for a person to use wrong terms in relation to carving was an unpardonable affront to etiquette. Carving all kinds of small birds was called *to thy* them; a quail, to *wing* it; a pheasant, to *allay* it; a duck, to *embrace* it; a hen, to *spoil* her; a goose, to *tare* her, and a list of similar technicalities too long and too ridiculous to repeat.

"Dr. Johnson said that 'You should praise, not ridicule, your friend who carves with as much earnestness of purpose as though he were legislating.' "

Here is how to carve a turkey:

Place bird with legs to right of carver. Remove leg (drumstick and thigh); hold drumstick end with left hand and cut through skin, drawing knife in right hand from left to right. Press leg away from turkey to platter with flat side of knife, then cut through remaining skin; transfer leg to side platter. Aim to remove oyster, choice dark meat, in spoon-shaped bone at the back with leg.

Hold leg at almost right angles to the plate; remove triangular piece of meat cutting down to joint. Serve as one, or cut to make two pieces.

Slice leg meat toward plate, circling the leg so that slices are uniform. Straddle thigh bone with fork, then cut lengthwise strips parallel to bone.

Remove wing; insert knife at point on breast about 1½ inches from wing. Cut through breast at a 45-degree angle down through joint to platter.

Slice breast meat. With the tip of the knife at the neck, begin near the bottom of the breast by making downward diagonal slices. Start each cut higher on the breast, keeping slices thin.

How to Truss a Turkey

Some people find that this is essential to their enjoyment of the day. It is more ritual than necessity. Others accomplish the same goal—holding the stuffing in the turkey—by means of skewers and clamps.

An upholsterer's needle 6 to 8 inches long threaded with a yard of cord is the equipment for trussing. A darning needle may be inserted into the opposite side by inserting hand in cavity.

Insert needle through cavity, between drumsticks, and bring out at same position on opposite side. Leave 3 to 4 inches of cord extending on near side where needle was originally inserted for a knot to be tied later.

Insert needle down through wing, draw string over back, then up through second wing. Cut cord.

Tie knot, drawing cord snugly to pull drumsticks toward breast. Insert needle through drumstick ends, then bring down and around body, inserting into bird through bone just above tail. Remove needle, leaving 6 inches of cord. Insert stuffing through rear opening. Draw cord tightly to pull drumsticks snugly to tail. This closes the opening without need of skewers or sewing unless opening is too large.

Plump breast end with stuffing, then fold neck skin under cord over back. Fasten skin to back with skewer.

On Etiquette

According to early New England Thanksgiving table etiquette, napkins were tucked under chins, and eating with one's knife was considered perfectly polite.

On Women Carvers

In the 19th century women were expected to carve the turkey. Sarah Hale recommended that "ladies ought especially to make a carving study and . . . perform the task allotted to them to prevent remark . . ." The tradition of assigning this task to the male head of household came later, as did the European custom of feeding oneself with a fork.

On Basting

The biggest fear of cooks is a dry turkey. Basting is often the culprit. Constant opening of the oven lets in dry air and slows roasting. Basting itself is a wasted effort because the skin of the bird is waterproof and sheds all the extra fat to the bottom of the roasting pan. Since cooks like to interact with their turkeys, and basting juices just roll off the skin, try a one-time glaze. For a dark golden skin, brush with equal parts molasses and soy sauce about an hour before end of cooking.

Napping—What We Do Best
on Thanksgiving

"Thankfulness took the form of rest. The old people dozed, careful householder and busy matron let go the reins of care, and children dreamily floated through the afternoon hours of this memorial day. Nature herself seemed to abet their mood, and to mellow the atmosphere both indoors and out. The happy season was lengthened by withholding of candles, and the brightness of sunset filled the room like a benediction."

—Thanksgiving Dinners, from "Old Time Child Life," late 19th century, E.H. Arr

POSED WITH THE query of why 167.723 million Americans nap after Thanksgiving dinner on many occasions, the National Turkey Federation has come up with a scientific answer. Here 'tis:

"Many people report drowsiness after eating Thanksgiving dinner.

"Recent studies suggest that the composition of a meal (particularly the ratio of carbohydrate to protein)

influences the production of brain neurotransmitters which are involved in sleep, mood and depression.

"Neurotransmitters in the brain are produced by the amino acid, tryptophan. A carbohydrate-rich—not a protein-rich—meal increases the level of tryptophan in the brain.

"Since many people eat an unusually large, many-coursed, carbohydrate-rich meal at Thanksgiving, they often associate the drowsiness they feel with the turkey. To be more accurate, they should associate their sleepy feelings to the increased amount of carbohydrates consumed."

Various and Sundry Thanksgiving Tinkerings, Tidbits and Trivia

" 'Twas founded be th' Puritans to give thanks f'r bein'
presarved fr'm th' Indyans, an' ... we keep it to give thanks we
are presarved fr'm th' Puritans."

—Finley Peter Dunne, *"Thanksgiving," Mr. Dooley's Opinions,*
1900

THANKSGIVING IS NOT without its oddments, quirks
and curiosities. Here is a selection having to do with all
things Thanksgiving, from cranberries to a mother who
charges her family for Thanksgiving dinner.

Catering Costs. In 1978 there must have been
some slow news days, because someone at the *Wichita*
(Kansas) *Eagle-Beacon* decided to ask a local caterer how
much it would cost at then-current prices to replicate the original Thanksgiving dinner, complete with eel, for 145 folks, a few more than were probably at the original feast. Estimate: $23,000, including spirits.

The Cranberry Bounce. The fresh cranberries you buy in the fall have proven their high quality—by bouncing! During preliminary grading in the plant, each cranberry is given seven chances to bounce over a wooden barrier four inches high. If the berry doesn't have bounce, it's discarded.

Doing Something Right. The price of *one* Thanksgiving dinner with all the trimmings in 1939 was $1.15, based on a sample meal. With a few minor substitutions based on changing tastes, a similar calculation yielded a price of $2.74 in 1993. The price of a restaurant Thanksgiving dinner has gone up approximately tenfold in that same period of time.

Doubling Up. In 1950, one of those unusual years with five Thursdays in November, the governor of Texas declared two Thanksgivings (the fourth and fifth Thursdays). "Texas," said the governor, "has enough to be thankful for to have two Thanksgiving Days."

Executive Bird. In April 1980 a wild turkey found its way onto the White House grounds in Washington and perched on a limb 70 feet above the ground in one of the American elms on the front lawn. According to one news account, it "set off some massive birdwatching among the White House staffers and launched a tidal wave of bad jokes." Later, as she strutted on the grounds outside the Oval Office, the *Washington Star* noted, "There's no getting away from the kind of symbolism a president would just as soon do without during an election year." The bird was presumed to have come from nearby Rock Creek Park, where wild turkeys are still found, and was returned there.

Export. In 1844 a barrel of cranberries en route to an American visitor in Hamburg was liberated in a shipwreck off the coast of Holland. The barrel floated to the island of Terschelling, where it was found by a beachcomber named Jan Sipkes Cupido. He was disappointed at the contents and scattered them over the ground, taking the barrel only. Floods later washed the cranberries into low areas where they took root and flourished. Cranberries still grow on Terschelling—but refuse to grow in any other place in Holland.

Family Matters. Miss Manners got a letter from the daughter of a woman who, following her divorce, had taken to charging $10 a head for family members to have Thanksgiving dinner. Miss Manners (Judith Martin), in her nationally syndicated column, lambasted the mother for charging and the daughter for not helping out in the first place.

Fish/Fowl. According to an article entitled "The Night I Shaved the Turkey and Other Harrowing Tales of Thanksgiving Disaster" in the November 1994 issue of *Yankee Magazine*, in 1950 there was a short-lived fad to fatten turkeys on a diet of fish. "It looked beautiful on the table," wrote a reader of the magazine who was at his parents' house on Thanksgiving, 1950, "but when my dad cut into it, it smelled like mackerel and tasted like cod liver oil." The reader, Thomas H. McNamara of Marshfield, Massachusetts, added, "I believe that 1950 was the one and only year that turkeys were fed a diet of fish."

Giving Him the Bird. Since 1948 the National Turkey Federation has presented a live turkey and two dressed turkeys every year to the President of the United States. In recent years the trend has been for the White House to grant the bird a "pardon" and give its live turkey to a zoo or children's farm. President Clinton's 1993 turkey escaped the table and was sent to Kidwell Farm in Herndon, Virginia. Its immediate role was to pose with kids wanting a picture of themselves with the First Turkey. Animal rights advocates support the act but object to the use of the word pardon. "What's he being pardoned for?" asks an official of People for the Ethical Treatment of Animals in a letter to the *Montgomery Journal* (Maryland). "The bird didn't embezzle or commit heresy."

The Guinness Book of Turkey Records. According to the National Turkey Federation: Leacroft Turkeys Ltd. of Petersborough, United Kingdom, raised the world's heaviest turkey, which topped the scales at 86 pounds. . . . American households consume turkey more often as a sandwich than any other way, with sandwiches accounting for 44% of all turkey consumption. . . . In 1994, about 300 million turkeys were raised. The National Turkey Federation "guesstimates" that 45 million of those turkeys were eaten at Thanksgiving, 22 million at Christmas, and 19 million at Easter. . . . In 1993, per capita consumption of turkey was 17.8 pounds compared to 10.5 pounds in 1980, a 70 percent increase. In 1994, 46 percent of American homes served turkey in some form once every two weeks all year long. That's up 35% from five years prior.

Inflation. A copy of the original Thanksgiving proclamation dated October 3, 1789, and issued by George Washington for November 26, 1789, was lost for more than a hundred years. In 1921 it showed up in a New York auction house where it was purchased by the Library of Congress for a price that was thought of as astonishing at the time: $300. Another original version of the proclamation came to light in 1989, at which time the value was estimated at between $80,000 and $100,000.

Keeping Busy. In 1901 President Theodore Roosevelt scarcely bothered to gulp his turkey. He had what the *Washington Post* termed "a busy day" on Thanksgiving. T.R. in 24 hours accomplished the following: Appointed a consul general and an assistant surgeon; announced he'd reduce duty of Cuban sugar; conferred with the heads of the National Retail Liquor Association, the National Irrigation Association, the Maimed Veterans Association, the past commander of the New York GAR, the Reform League of Baltimore, the pastor of the New York Fifth Avenue Presbyterian Church (to discuss "religious work in the Army"), the head of the Gold Standard Committee, a Senator from Indiana, and two Senators from Wisconsin—while Sir Henry Wrenfordsley, described as a "member of the Carlton Club," and Bishop John Walden dropped in for a chat!

Lunar Lunch. When Neil Armstrong and Edwin Aldrin sat down to eat their first meal on the moon, their foil-wrapped food packets contained roasted turkey and all the trimmings.

National Dinner. In 1962 Massachusetts strongly proposed a National Thanksgiving Dinner that would have the President consume an official, legislated meal. "The President lights the National Christmas Tree, and throws out the first baseball—maybe we can persuade him to pass the first drumstick on an annual basis," said the director of the Plymouth area Chamber of Commerce.

Next! Prozac for Pilgrims? A consumer group, the Public Health Research Group, in the early 1980s claimed that the manufacturer of the tranquilizer Librium was exploiting Thanksgiving by featuring Pilgrims in ads which suggested the drug was something the world should be thankful for.

Ostrich on the Menu. 1994 marked the debut of an effort by American ostrich farmers to get their bird, which averages 7 feet tall and 300 pounds, on people's Thanksgiving Day menu.

Ranking. In 1994 Hallmark reported that Thanksgiving as a card-sending occasion ranked seventh behind Christmas, Valentine's Day, Easter, Mother's Day, Father's Day, and graduation. Halloween was in 9th place.

Why is Thanksgiving ranked so low? Perhaps because so many people go home for Thanksgiving, requiring fewer cards.

Rumored. The costume that Big Bird wears on *Sesame Street* is rumored to be made of turkey feathers.

Soft Touch. It was late in the cold afternoon of Thanksgiving Day, 1887, in the gymnasium of the Gothic building housing the Farragut Boat Club at the edge of Lake Michigan in Chicago in the 3000 block of Lake Park Avenue.

A group of 20 or so young men had gathered there for the reading of a series of telegrams that would reveal the progress and final score of the Harvard-Yale football game. Small wagers were made between telegrams.

These were single young men with simple honest jobs. Among others assembled here were a cashier, Frank Staples; a bookkeeper, Carl Bryant; a salesman, Ogden Downs; and a watchman, Edward Palmer.

When the final score was announced—Yale 17, Harvard 8—bets were paid off and as one historian of the moment put it, "Animal spirits came to the fore. Horseplay was rampant."

At one moment during all of this, one of the Yale boosters picked up a stray boxing glove and lobbed it across the gym at one of the Harvard fans. The target saw the glove coming, grabbed a pole and whacked it back across the room over the pitcher's head. The batsman howled with glee.

Seeing this, a young reporter for the Chicago Board of Trade named George Hancock said, "I've got it. Let's play ball." Hancock shaped and bound the glove in its own laces so that it resembled a ball and then chalked out a crude diamond on the gym floor. The dimensions were smaller to fit the confines of the gym. The broom handle was broken off to form a bat.

Teams were chosen and play began. Time has obscured the score of that first game—each team scored more than 40 runs—and no record remains of how the teams were determined, although it has always been assumed that they were divided between followers of the Crimson and the Blue. This odd game of "scrub" baseball lasted for more than an hour.

It might have ended there if George Hancock—who had been thinking about this game since they had started to play—hadn't gathered the lads around him and made a little speech. "I believe this affair can be worked into a regular game of baseball which can be played indoors," he said, "and if you come down Saturday night I'll make up some rules and have a ball and bat which will suit the purpose of the sport and do no damage to the surroundings."

That was the beginning of the game of softball.

Stuff This. This item appeared on the "kid's page" in *The St. Petersburg Times* for Monday, November 21, 1994. It is presented as a possible justification for keeping children out of the kitchen.

Top 10 Alternative Turkey Stuffings

Pez
Nickelodeon Gack
Spaghetti-Os
Leftover Halloween candy corn
Duncan Hines ready-made frosting *and* peanut butter
Fried squid rings
Tater Tots

Cheez Whiz
Chocolate-flavored Cool Whip
Pizza-flavored Combos!

Mmmmm. . . . MOM!

Talking Turkey. Only tom turkeys (males) gobble. Hen turkeys (females) make a clicking noise.

Tattooed Bird. In 1887, the Grover Clevelands carved a turkey given to the White House by Albe T. Hillard from North Stonington, Conn. It was described as a "beauty of exceedingly large proportions and finely moulded with a skin of purest tint." On one side was the monogram of the President, on the other side the initials of both raiser and shipper. This work was done by pricking the flesh with hot needles, an idea which originated in the head of a North Stonington schoolmarm.

Thanksgiving at the Movies? Humbug! Think about it! Recent years have seen Hollywood turn on Thanksgiving dinner and use it as a metaphor for chaos and disaster. A few examples suffice. In 1987 there was *Planes Trains and Automobiles*, in which Steve Martin and John Candy link up on a wild goose chase to get home for Thanksgiving. Martin's character doesn't make it. Very funny—as one reviewer pointed out at the time, Martin and Candy could make a reading of the phone book funny—but it is really a movie about Thanksgiving misery. Another is Barry Levinson's marvelous 1990 immigrant's tale, *Avalon*, with the disastrous Thanksgiving dinner in which all hell breaks loose when the narrator's Uncle Jules shows up late for Thanksgiving and the turkey is carved without him. Another 1990 film was entitled *Thanksgiving Day* and is a black comedy about a family's attempt to deal with the fact that the father, played by Tony Curtis, keels over and dies of a heart attack while carving the Thanksgiving turkey. This movie was made for television. There's more. *Scent of a Woman* in 1992 starred Al Pacino as retired Lt. Col. Frank Slade, and Chris O'Donnell as a student taking care of the blind Colonel to make extra money over Thanksgiving weekend. Great film but horrendous Thanksgiving dinner scene.

This is not to say that Thanksgiving has fared well in earlier times. Back in 1952 there was a turkey called *Plymouth Adventure* starring Spencer Tracy, which reduced the whole story of the Pilgrims and the *Mayflower* to that of a second-rate soap opera.

Turkey Feather Lore. It's estimated that turkeys have approximately 3,500 feathers at maturity. The bulk of turkey feathers are disposed of; however, some feathers may be used for special purposes. For instance, dyed feathers are used to make American Indian costumes or as quills for pens. Turkey feather down has been used to make pillows. For commercial use, turkey skins are tanned and used to make items such as cowboy boots, belts and other accessories.

Turkey in the Shell. Americans have found all sorts of odd ways to cook their turkeys, some as bizarre as Dave Barry's tongue-in-cheek suggestion for last-minute turkey zapped with a blow torch. Over time they have been put in dishwashers, bagged in paper and draped over the hot manifolds of cars and trucks. The oddest fad was one that asked the cook to encase the bird in a paste of flour and water. In a Thanksgiving 1994 article on cooking techniques, Janice Okun, food editor of the *Buffalo News*, notes that the flour and water treatment required extensive "use of a mallet in order to get to the meat."

War Bird. In 1969, 2,337,645 pounds of turkey were ordered for the troops in Vietnam for Thanksgiving.

Winging It. Domesticated turkey strains have been bred to produce lots of meat and cannot fly. Wild turkeys can fly for short distances up to 55 miles per hour and can run 25 miles per hour.

Worst Poem. There has been lots of bad Thanksgiving poetry but it would be hard to beat "The Night Before Thanksgiving" by Eva Lovett Carson, of which only the first few lines are repeated here.

> " 'Twas the night before Thanksgiving,
> And the turkeys that were living
> Sat a-mourning in the hen-house for the turkeys that lay
>   dead,
> For the dawning of the morrow,
> That to them brought only sorrow,
> To the inmates of the farm-house brought a jolly time
>   instead."

Hold on! Here is one that is even more ghastly:

> "Turkey meets us
>   every year
> With his message
>   of good cheer
> And to meet him
>   is a treat
> When he treats us
>   with his meat on Thanksgiving."

Ye Eggs. Turkey eggs, slightly larger than jumbo chicken eggs, occasionally may be purchased at health food stores or at farm markets. They are not a common retail item. Even though excellent for cooking and nutritious, they are expensive, costing about 75 cents per egg. The majority of turkey eggs are used to support turkey production.

Yukon Gold. In *The Gold Rush*, in 1925, nostalgia for the holiday inspired the famous scene in which Charlie Chaplin tries to create a celebration in difficult circumstances. On Thanksgiving Day, he is trapped in a blizzard in a cabin in the Yukon, with no food. He stews his boot, then sits down to savor it with dignity, twirling the laces on the tines of his fork like spaghetti, gnawing the cobbler's nails as if they were bones.

_____

_____

MULTICULTURAL ASPECTS OF THANKSGIVING

"As we remember the faith and values that made America great, we should recall that our tradition of Thanksgiving is older than our nation itself. Indeed, the native American Thanksgiving antedated those of the new Americans. In the words of the eloquent Seneca traditions of the Iroquois, 'Give it your thought, that with one mind we may now give thanks to Him our creator.'"

> —Ronald Reagan in his 1984 Thanksgiving Proclamation

AT THANKSGIVING TIME in 1949, a group of American legislators met with Pope Pius XII in the Vatican. The Pope commented favorably on the American holiday and suggested that it become a universal day of thanks.

Although a lot was made of the comment at the time—"Pope Suggests World Observe America's Thanksgiving Day" was a typical newspaper headline—nothing came of it.

But the idea begged the question in the sense that there is some kind of thanksgiving associated with so many cultures and nations, although many of these festivals are historic and no longer observed.

There are, in fact, so many precedents that one is hard-pressed to know where to start. The Chinese observed rites of thanksgiving thousands of years ago. Thanksgiving can be traced back to the ancient Jewish Feast of Tabernacles. The ancient Greeks held a feast to honor Demeter, goddess of agriculture.

There are many other celebrations. In his book *The Golden Bough*, Sir James G. Frazer tells of a number, including a Lithuanian harvest feast typical of the ancient European thanksgiving tradition. At the time of the autumn sowing, the farmer would gather nine handfuls of each grain that he had grown, making them into bread and beer. A chicken and a hen were killed and cooked in a new pot. Prayers were said, and the bread, beer, and poultry were all consumed at one ceremony-laden feast.

Following a traditional autumn feast of the Druids, the Anglo-Saxons held their "harvest home" celebration, the high point of the year in rural districts, which is still observed in one way or another in parts of the British Isles. These were peasant festivals for which the symbol was the cornucopia (horn of plenty). In Scotland, such a gathering was called a "kern"; often after a special service at the church, which was decorated with autumn flowers, fruits, and vegetables, a harvest feast was served to all attendants.

On special occasions, England celebrated days of thanksgiving; for example, in 1356, after Edward the Black Prince had defeated the French, and in 1588, following the victory over the Spanish Armada. Also, for more than two hundred years the British observed a day of gratitude for the failure of the famous Gunpowder Plot in 1605. Other countries besides England have had thanksgiving celebrations in the fall, including Russia, Poland, and Sweden.

There were and are native American Indian thanksgivings that predate, parallel and came after the event in Plymouth—clearly showing that thanksgiving was and is an Indian celebration.

Where to start?

Not only did the Indians celebrate their own Thanksgiving, but they grabbed onto the one of the colonists. In what amounts to the first newspaper printed in America, *Publick Occurrences both Foreign and Domestic* for Thursday, Sept. 25, 1690, published in Boston, the following appears on page one: "The Christianized *Indians* in some part of *Plimouth*, have newly appointed a day of Thanksgiving to God for his mercy in supplying their extream and pinching Necessities under their late want of Corn, and for His giving them now a prospect of a very *Comfortable Harvest*. This example may be worth Mentioning."

The Pueblo tribes in the Southwest practiced corn dances in which they give thanks for the year's crop. The Seneca observed a nine-day thanksgiving observance in the spring. Few, if any, tribes lacked some ceremony that did not express a sense of thanksgiving.

Barnabas Skiuhushu, President of the Indian Association of America, wrote to the *New York Times* in a letter published on Thanksgiving Day, 1936, and said it as clearly as anyone has ever said it ever since: "The American Indian was noted for his strict observance of Thanksgiving Days for many centuries before the arrival of the white man in America."

Despite and because of this, there has been friction between the two traditions. Beginning in 1969, and for a number of years thereafter, local tribes gathered in Plymouth around the statue of Massasoit, the chief of the Wampanoag who welcomed the original Pilgrims. In 1969 a spokesman for the United American Indians of New England led 300 people on a Thanksgiving Day fast, insisting "Indians have nothing to be thankful for." In 1970 Indian demonstrators were removed from *Mayflower II* in Plymouth harbor by police. There have been other demonstrations, native American alternative marches to the Macy's Thanksgiving Parade and some words of precise and prolonged anger. "It is their holiday, not ours" was one of the mildest things uttered by an angry Indian about the Thanksgiving festival.

The point is well taken.

Increasingly, public schools are using Thanksgiving as a time to acknowledge Indian customs and history. On Thanksgiving, 1994, the *Washington Post* published an article on the Indianization of Thanksgiving, describing how the holiday was now seen as a moment to shine a positive light on native Americans. "This is the teaching of Thanksgiving 1990s style," said Sari Horwitz of the paper. "Sure, students learn about Pilgrims and turkeys and pumpkin pie. But teachers in the District, and across the country, say they are using Thanksgiving to teach lessons on Indians, a minority group that most children hear little about."

Some traditionalists have despaired of this, but the fact is we have used Indians wrongly on Thanksgiving and are now beginning to balance the scales.

We have used the Indians as the majority culture has needed during our ever-changing observation of Thanksgiving. According to Jim Baker of Plimoth Plantation, during the period of and just after the Indian Wars of the 19th century the Indians were depicted as hostile. More than one illustrator used in his Thanksgiving theme a Pilgrim hat with an arrow in it. If this sounds dreadfully old-fashioned and 19th-century, consider the fact that until a few years ago the symbol for the Massachusetts Turnpike was a Pilgrim hat (with its mandatory buckle) with an arrow through it. The arrow has been removed, but the unfounded hint of hostility remains.

Canadian Thanksgiving. The only modern Thanksgiving that is close to the American version is the Canadian Thanksgiving, which has many of the same trappings as the U.S. version including turkey and cranberries. In Canada, Thanksgiving is proclaimed annually as "a day of General Thanksgiving to Almighty God for the bountiful harvest with which Canada has been blessed."

Canadian Thanksgiving draws upon many of the same traditions that the U.S. observance does. One of them is the harvest celebrations in European peasant societies; another is formal observances in the land which is now Canada, such as the thanksgiving celebrated by Martin Frobisher in the eastern Arctic in 1578—the first North American Thanksgiving, according to the Canadians.

But they also acknowledge the Pilgrims' celebration of their first harvest in Massachusetts (1621) involving the uniquely American dishes of turkey, squash, and pumpkin. According to the *Canadian Encyclopedia*, the celebration was brought to Nova Scotia in the 1750s, and the citizens of Halifax commemorated the end of the French and Indian or Seven Years' War (1763) with a day of Thanksgiving. Loyalists brought the celebration to other parts of the country.

In 1879 the Parliament in Ottawa declared November 6 as a day of Thanksgiving; it was celebrated as a national rather than a religious holiday. Later and earlier dates were observed in other years, the most popular being the third Monday in October. It was not until January 31, 1957, that Parliament proclaimed the observance of Thanksgiving on the second Monday in October, where it remains to this day.

Yankee Claims and Southern Stakes

"... the act of giving thanks; the acknowledgment of favors or benefits; an utterance (as a prayer) that is offered in a set form of words and that expresses gratitude especially for divine goodness and mercies; or a day appointed for such a celebration."

—From the definition of "thanksgiving" in *Webster's Third New International Dictionary* (1961)

THE FIRST WORDS of John F. Kennedy's 1963 Thanksgiving proclamation, which was written before his assassination and released by President Lyndon B. Johnson, were these: "Over three centuries ago, our forefathers in Virginia and Massachusetts, far from home in a lonely wilderness, set aside a time of thanksgiving."

There was a special reason for the phrasing. President Kennedy in his 1961 and 1962 proclamations credited Massachusetts Pilgrims with the first Thanksgiving Day observance.

This aroused a legitimate claim of foul from Virginia, whose spokesman, State Senator John J. Wicker, pointed out that in 1619—on Dec. 14—a group of settlers landed at Berkeley Hundred on the James River and offered the first Thanksgiving. Wicker persisted and made his case directly to the White House. In late December 1962, Arthur Schlesinger, Jr., Kennedy's special assistant, thereupon acknowledged Virginia's claim, pleading as excuse for the gaffe "the unconquerable New England bias on the part of the White House staff." A year later President Kennedy's message began with a reference to "our forefathers in Virginia and Massachusetts."

This was neither the first, nor will it be the last, time that claims have been made to the contrary, and presidents now tend to credit everyone but the Vikings, whose credit is still forthcoming. Listen to these words from Ronald Reagan's 1985 proclamation:

> "A band of settlers arriving in Maine in 1607 held a service of thanks for their safe journey, and 12 years later settlers in Virginia set aside a day of thanksgiving for their survival. In 1621, Gov. William Bradford created the most famous of all such observances at Plymouth Colony when a bounteous harvest prompted him to proclaim a special day 'to render Thanksgiving to the almighty God for all his blessings.' The Spaniards in California and the Dutch in New Amsterdam also held services to give public thanks to God."

Here are the possibilities in chronological order:

June 30, 1564: A small group of French Huguenots settled near what is now Jacksonville, Florida, and were wiped out by a Spanish raiding party within a year. However, on arriving, their leader recorded, "We sang a psalm of Thanksgiving unto God, beseeching Him that it would please Him to continue His accustomed goodness towards us."

May 27, 1578: The first known thanksgiving service held in what is now Canada was conducted on the coast of Newfoundland when the Rev. Mr. Wolfall, chaplain of the Frobisher expedition, expressed gratitude for the "adventure" and for a safe voyage.

April 20, 1598: There are Texans who claim that the first thanksgiving was held by a group of Spanish colonists who held a big thanksgiving feast. The event occurred as a 400-member party traveled from what is now Chihuahua State in Mexico to the area near what is now Santa Fe, N.M. The trek was recorded in detail by Capt. Gaspar Perez de Villagra, who noted that the party ran out of water five days before reaching the Rio Grande River. The horses were crazy with thirst. He said that when the party finally spotted the river, men and horses plunged in and drank their fill.

After 10 days of hunting, fishing and recuperating, the captain wrote, "We built a great bonfire and roasted the meat and fish, and then all sat down to a repast the like of which we had never enjoyed before. We were happy that our trials were over; as happy as were the passengers in the ark when they saw the dove returning with the olive branch in his beak, bringing tidings that the deluge had subsided."

Dr. W. H. Timmons, a historian at the University of Texas in El Paso, noted to a reporter from the *New York Times* that the account did not mention a thanksgiving mass, "but you know they had to be thankful for surviving."

One of those supporting this claim is Sheldon Hall, a Spanish history buff who traces his own ancestry to the Pilgrims and says that the feast of thanksgiving featured a play in which the soldiers depicted the group's success. It was, Hall claims, the first play staged in the Americas.

April 29, 1607: Colonists at Cape Henry, Va., celebrate a thanksgiving.

August 9, 1607: Settlers at the short-lived Popham Colony, at the mouth of the Kennebec River in what is now Maine, celebrate thanksgiving. The account itself, as given in "A Relation of a Voyage to Sagadahoc," is as follows: "Sondaye beinge the 9th of August, in the morninge the most part of our holl company of both our shipes landed on this Illand, whear the crosse standeth; and thear we heard a sermon delyvred unto us by our preacher, gyvinge God thanks for our happy metinge and saffe aryvall into the contry; and so retorned abord aggain." Rev. Richard Seymour, the preacher, was an Episcopalian, and the passage shows that he adhered to the custom of his church. The Puritan thanksgiving day was a weekday observance, and quite another thing in its whole temper.

This was an early attempt at settlement by the Plymouth Company but was abandoned within the year. In her book, *Thanksgiving: An American Holiday, An American History*, Diana Karter Appelbaum points out, "Such spontaneous thanksgiving services for deliverance from danger were common in that pious age."

So little was accomplished at this colony that cynics have suggested that the only thing that Mainers could claim for this attempt at settlement was "the first Thanksgiving."

December 14, 1619: Thanksgiving was declared an annual holiday at Berkeley Hundred, the site that would be known as the Berkeley Plantation on the James River in Virginia. The first observation took place with colonists under the leadership of Capt. John Woodliffe who arrived on the ship *Margaret* and gave thanks for their safe deliverance from the perils of the sea.

What is impressive about this first full proclamation is that it called for thanksgiving as an annual event: "Impr wee ordaine that the day of our ships arrivall at the place assigned for plantaçon in the land of Virginia shall be yearly and perputualy keept holy as a day of thanksgiving to Almighty god." Richard L. Morton, author of the book *Colonial Virginia*, in helping to make the claim for Virginia in 1967, told the Associated Press, "What interests me is that this observance was to be a perennial thing, not just one little Thanksgiving."

It did not, however, work out as perennial. The Berkeley Thanksgiving tradition was continued for three years but ended abruptly on Good Friday 1622 when the colony was wiped out in the first great Indian massacre.

The Berkeley Thanksgiving had faded into oblivion until State Senator Wicker, of Richmond, discovered a reference to the Virginia observation when doing research for a speech. Wicker formed a Virginia Thanksgiving Festival, which has marked the event each year on the first Sunday in November. The date of the landing was December 14, but the weather is likely to be better in early November.

This Virginia Thanksgiving was revived again in 1958, and is now celebrated in special events and reenactments at a Virginia Thanksgiving Festival on 1,400 acres of plantation grounds about 30 miles west of Williamsburg.

Berkeley Plantation was built in 1726 by Benjamin Harrison, a leader in colonial affairs, and the "founding father" of a family that, like the Adams family and later the Kennedy family, played a significant role in the political life of the nation. But even before the mansion was built, the Berkeley Hundred played a role in many phases of American life. For instance, America's first Bourbon whiskey was made there in 1621 or 1622. A "brew of corn and maize was much better than British ale," an Episcopalian clergyman noted. The plantation mansion today is furnished superbly in period pieces that evoke the colonial days of its greatest glory. It is said to be the oldest three-story brick house in the country. Also to be seen are traditional terraced boxwood gardens.

October 15, 1621: The Pilgrims of Plymouth celebrate their first harvest festival in the New World, now commonly regarded as the "First Thanksgiving."

1623: The Pilgrims of Plymouth celebrate what they would call their first day of thanksgiving, a religious day of thanks. To the Pilgrims, a day of thanksgiving was a highly religious day, marked by attendance at church, prayers, and probably fasting. In contrast, they considered a harvest festival to be a leisure activity—perhaps as much as three days devoted to feasting and games.

Winter 1637: The Dutch on Manhattan Island held a "Thanks Day." It was called to celebrate the massacre of hundreds of Pequot Indians. In 1936, Barnabas Skiuhushu, President of the Indian Association of America, recalled this horrible celebration in a long letter to the *New York Times*: "The most unfortunate fact about the historical background is that many Thanksgiving Days proclaimed since [this] first one in 1637 were to give thanks for some bloody military victory over the Indians, the French or the English."

All of this gets a bit tedious after a bit, and the motives of those arguing one site over another as the "authentic" site become suspect. In 1990 the

Quincy (Massachusetts) *Patriot-Ledger* sent a reporter to Plymouth to sort out the Texas claim, and the first sentence of her report was this: "PLYMOUTH— When a Texas town sought to wrest the credit for the first Thanksgiving from Plymouth last week, residents in both communities cited tourism dollars as a key benefit to the claim."

WHY WE LOVE THANKSGIVING

"Thanksgiving is a state of mind."

—Title of painting depicting a typically American
Thanksgiving (ca. 1950)

IT IS THE most relaxed and least threatening of holidays
in the sense that we don't have to worry about religious
differences, politics, gift giving, or redemption.

Of all the holy days—or what we now call holidays—it is secular and religious at the same time. It is
part of all religions, owned by all, owned by no one in
particular.

It is the only holiday that condones and encourages
napping on the couch.

Of all the words we can hear, few are as nice as "I'll be home for
Thanksgiving," or "The turkey is ready to carve," or "The kids are here," or
"Can I interest anyone in leftovers?"

It is a great day for parades, especially for those of us who love immense
floating cartoon characters—Bullwinkles and Barneys large enough to blot out
the sun—and the play-by-play commentary on the far-flung marching bands
and twirling units who held bake sales and car washes to pay for the trip.

We love to hear Willard Scott proclaim from under a heavy coat and muffler, "This is the prettiest day you're ever going to want to see."

Of all the smells known to humankind, the most delightful of all are the smells of Thanksgiving. There are few of us to whom these smells do not, at once, trigger a wonderful sense of nostalgia and summon up a great hunger.

It is the day that celebrates neighborhoods and family traditions, from secret stuffing ingredients to touch-football extravaganzas inevitably called the Turkey Bowl.

Of all the holidays, it is the only one that immediately embraces immigrants and foreign visitors. Families from elsewhere love to tell about their first Thanksgiving, and there is a great body of family lore concerning American turkey and improvised stuffing of ravioli, fried rice, or a dozen other possibilities. Ethnic restaurants close on Thanksgiving so the owners and employees can go home and cook turkey.

It is the only holiday that asks us to do something for those less fortunate than ourselves. This is the day when we are most likely to hear that the Presidential family opened the day working in a soup kitchen before heading off to Camp David.

Of all the times of the year, it is the one time when we brag about the ordeal of travel and one's ability to deal with "the busiest travel day of the year." Overcoming this to get home is a badge of honor and has nothing to do with the kind of complaining that commuters indulge in.

It is a festival of foods that are singularly American: sweet potatoes and brown sugar, mashed potatoes, creamed onions, cranberry sauce, roasted turkey, giblet gravy, cornbread stuffing, soft dinner rolls, and apples or pumpkin in cinnamon-spiced pies. The amount of starch and the excess of sugar in this one meal bewilders Europeans, but delights Americans. It is a time to catch Julia Child on television and while away your time chatting on the Butterball Turkey Talk Line and other 800 numbers posted on refrigerator doors since last year.

Finally, in a world of constant change, it changes little.

Listen to the words of 19th-century writer E.H. Arr in an essay entitled *Old Time Child Life*, writing about the New England Thanksgiving of earlier days: "Next to the religious aspect of this day, its best essence has always been its hospitality. It is the home-rallying point of disintegrated families,— the altar from which the incense of affection goes up with that of baked meats, and kindleth anew from its yearly gathering of forces. 'Going home to Thanksgiving' is the watchword of many old New England families; and with them, for that day at least, the current of love flows backward to the fathers and mothers and the dear old grandparents, who sit waiting by ancestral hearths."

"Mankind is never truly thankful for the benefits of life until they have experienced the want of them."

—Attributed to an Army surgeon at Valley Forge,
national day of Thanksgiving, 1789